WHAT WE TALK ABOUT WHEN WE TALK ABOUT BRAINS

WHAT WE TALK ABOUT WHEN WE TALK ABOUT BRAINS

THE RED RAIN STORIES

PETER M. BALL

GenrePunk Books (an imprint of Brain Jar Press)
PO Box 6687
Upper Mt Gravatt, QLD, 4122
Australia
GenrePunk Books: www.PeterMBall.com
Brain Jar Press: www.BrainJarPress.com

Cover design by Brain Jar Press
Cover Image: Zombies illustration, Breakermaximus/Shutterstock

ISBN: 978-1-922479-77-8 (paperback) | 978-1-922479-76-1 (Ebook)

CONTENTS

OUT PAST THE FENCE

The storm crept up on them an hour before sunset, bringing wind and gusts of crimson rain. Janice was in the backyard, patching gaps in the barbed wire barricades protecting their house from wandering deaders. The perfect vantage point to observe the bats fleeing their colony by the river, launching and wheeling in a black-winged cloud. They dipped below the tree line and reappeared, beginning their evening migration early. Janice wiped her brow with one hand, watched the swirling bats disperse.

Out past the river, towards the beach, the rain was already thick and dark. A blackout curtain encroaching upon the shoreline, sweeping inland with a fury.

Janice sealed the tear in the fence, cinching the patch-job tight. Not perfect, but it would hold for a while, and she needed to secure the tanks before the rain's hit them and contaminated their drinking water. Up on the veranda, on the makeshift clothesline Val had built under the cover, the sheets and towels shimmied and danced in the wind. Janice ducked under them and took the shortest route to the water supply, hauled the seals over the tanks and diverted the water flow away. She made another trip to the shed and powered down their generator, gathering up the spare solar batteries they charged there to get them through the night.

The rain started as she made it back to the house, clattering up the back stairs at a trot. Janice waited at the back door, casting a quick glance at the sky. "Dinner in ten," she said. "If you're hungry."

Val went inside and washed up, sponging off the day's sweat with the water bucket tucked into the bathtub. Janice sang as she finished up in the kitchen, her sweet voice serenading the coming storm with an old Britney Spears song Val couldn't place. Then the storm hit with its full force, water splattering their windows like streaks of gore, downpour hammering the corrugated iron roof hard enough to drown out even the thunder.

They lit a lamp and ate without speaking, Val's attention absorbed in the battered book, Janice half-caught on the window and the storm beyond, worrying the half-patched fence line might not survive if the dead swarmed. It should hold. Dead were rare in their neck of the woods, even on during a red rain, and it would take over a dozen to pull the fence down without drawing attention from the house.

Still, she worried. Rare didn't mean never.

Janice ate mechanically, barely tasting the roasted beets, potatoes, and carrots pulled from Val's garden. The rain eased, and the deafening clatter overhead fell to a constant rumble. Janice glanced at the locker out in the hall, right beside the front door, and tried to remember whether the .303 or the 12 gauge had more ammunition. Once Val finished eating, Janice excused herself and returned the plates to the kitchen. She unlocked the gun cabinet and checked, assuring herself the .303 was the better choice, and carried two boxes of bullets out to the veranda to prepare.

Loading a fresh clip soothed the turmoil in Janice's gut. Val emerged halfway through the second reload, taking a position at the railing. She scowled at the fence line, long dress whipping in the wind. "You're going out again in the morning?"

Janice stilled her hands. She set the half-loaded clip on the arm of the chair and jerked her chin towards the river. "Storm like this is going to rile 'em up. Militia will need folks to help quell the latest outbreak."

Rain tapped at the corrugated iron, as though testing ways to get inside. The washing snapped and danced on the strong wind, trying to tear free of the pegs. The rain blew in, and Janice gnawed on her lip. It wouldn't take much to stain the sheets for good, rendering them unusable.

"Should they come in?"

"They're still wet," Val said.

"Worse than wet, if the wind picks up."

"Water doesn't blow in that far," Val said. "It's why I strung 'em up here, instead of using the line in the yard."

Lightning split the sky, way off in the distance. It flashed red during storms like this one, tainted. Val stepped back from the veranda rail, wiping hands against the yellow dress. "It feels like it's always storming, now. You're out with the militia every week, seems like."

"It is what it is," Janice said. "We don't control the weather."

"I know. I just…" Val huffed a frustrated breath. "I miss you when you're out there. I worry, all the time."

Janice set the ammo box on the floor and placed the clips beside it. Val stood facing the storm, hands caught in the loose fabric of her dress, twisting a curl around her finger. Janice came up behind and touched Val on the hip, rested chin against Val's shoulder.

"It's the season," she said. "It'll pass. It always does."

Val didn't move, body taut with worry. "It's not been long enough for us to say always yet."

"Okay, yeah. I'll give you that." Janice brushed Val's neck with her lips and felt Val's body shiver at the contact. The hand toying with the loose fabric stilled. "But this will pass soon, and I can spend more time at home. That's how it's gone for the last few years."

Val forced the nod, a small concession to Janice's logic. It was hot out, even with the storm. Red rains never did squat to drop the humidity, and they were both beaded with sweat.

"You want tea before you head out?" Val said. "I can make you thermos to get through the night."

"Deke and Cody will want me out there the moment the rain eases up." Janice reached around Val and hugged her tight. "No telling when they'll call, and I'd rather you got some shut-eye. I can wake you before I go. Make sure you're ready if something wanders close."

"Okay," Val said.

They stood there, hugging. Janice clasped both hands, resting them on Val's stomach, holding on as long as she could.

"Be careful," Val said.

"Always am."

Val turned, and they kissed. A perfunctory motion. Janice let go before Val could try to pull free. She went back to the .303 ammunition, preparing for the storm's aftermath. Val retreated into the house, cleaning up after dinner.

The house creaked and shuddered in the storm, but it would pass. The storms always passed.

The rain let up midmorning, but Janice wasn't back yet. Val sat on the front porch with the solar lamp and her book, enjoying the brief respite from the rain. Pretending she wasn't waiting for a lantern beam to appear on the curve of the road. The clouds had gathered again, heavy with rain yet to spill upon the earth. Deke and Cody, who ran the militia, would gather recruits to hold off the attacks following the storm.

No need to worry, yet. Plenty of reasons for Janice to come home late.

The militia ute came around the corner an hour after sunset, dropping Janice by the front gate. Val took up position with the shotgun, keeping watch as Janice undid the bicycle locks holding the first gate closed. Janice moved with practice ease, all too aware their entrances and exits presented the most dangerous parts of leaving the house. Val kept the shotgun against her shoulder, scanned the tree line over the road. There hadn't been deaders this far in for months, but better safe than sorry.

Janice unlocked the inner gate and slipped through the narrow opening. Val lowered the gun and helped fit the crossbar in place. Tension leached free of Janice's shoulders, and Val touched the sodden, cold flannel shirt with tentative fingers.

"We lost two people on Cove Road, trying to hold off a swarm coming through the bush," Janice said. "George was right beside me, when the deader got him. Came through the undergrowth, had him down before I realised they'd got close."

Val pulled Janice inside and closed the door behind them. She flipped the deadbolts and slid the bars in place, layers upon layers. Damp clothes left wet, red splotches on the kitchen linoleum, pink streaks darkening as the water pooled. Val slipped the .303 free of Janice's tight grip, returned it to the gun cabinet along with the shotgun. Val didn't move, jaw set in a hard line.

"George Vance or George Andrianakis?" Val said.

"George Sinclair. Old guy, pushing sixty." Janice shivered at the thought. "Used to bring those comic books to trade, after his son died a few years back."

"Who else?"

Janice shrugged and turned away. Val bit her tongue and considered the dripping shirt, the soft squelch when Janice shifted her weight. The wind blew across the fields outside, rustling through the scrub across the road. They should have cleared it back a little more, bought themselves more space to see the dead if they got this close.

Val pushed Janice towards the couch, pushed her down, and unlaced her boots. "You can't dwell on it too much," she said. "It's no good for your mental health."

Janice barked a short, mocking laugh.

"I'm serious," Val said.

"I know you are."

"Leave it out there, on the far side of the fence."

"I know." Janice placed a bare foot against the floor, wriggling toes against the hardwood. The rain started again, a light sprinkle easing in on the rippling wind. A greater storm loomed, awaiting its moment.

"I'm hungry," Janice said. "We got anything easy in the kitchen?"

"Wash up," Val said. "I'll make you something."

"I'm real hungry."

"You're also red," Val said. "Better to clean up before you eat."

Janice rolled her shoulders and stared down the hall, watching the red glow of the pot-bellied stove they'd set up in the first weeks. "I've had some water simmering," Val said. "Cleaning up will do you good."

Val counted the seconds before Janice agreed, trudging towards the bathroom. A concession driven by exhaustion rather than a shared belief hot water and a good scrub could remove the day's woes. Val retrieved the streaming water from the kitchen, emptied the pot and left Janice to handle the task of stripping off the damp clothes and washing herself down. Better to let Janice stew, prepare food and a cup of tea to help take the edge off the day.

The kitchen's warmth provided solace on days when they couldn't bridge the gap between those who stayed home and those who ventured forth. Val stirred soup and boiled water, readied both just as Janice re-appeared, dark hair damp and slicked against her skull, one faint crimson streak seeping forth, as though an old wound had begun to leak.

Val put the soup and the tea on the table. She collected a rag from the sink.

"Sit," she said. "You missed a spot."

She ran the cloth over the damp hair, soaked up the last red stain. Janice waited, still as the grave, one hand on her soup spoon. Began eating the moment Val broke contact, hunching low and scooping quick, tiny mouthfuls at a furious speed. She paused two-thirds of the way through the bowl and looked out the kitchen window. This side of the house looked out over the Williams family fields, still devoted to raising dairy cows despite the risks.

Janice said, "I didn't know the other guy the deaders ate. I think he was one of the Greys, out past Montville. Cody said he had three kids."

"Oh," Val said. "Oh no. That's awful."

Janice said nothing.

"At least you made it home," Val said. "I worry, when you're out there."

Janice shifted in her chair, rested her forearms against the table. "I wanted to stay out there longer, make sure we got them all. There's fresh rain coming in tonight, and there's good odds another swarm's coming. Plenty of us knew it, but Cody sent us home."

"That's good," Val said. "You all needed rest."

"That's what Cody said, but he's wrong." Janice scrubbed both hands through her damp hair. Her eyes brimmed, red and searching for solace. "George didn't die from the bite, Val. He kept breathing and he knew he got bit and he couldn't bring himself to do what he needed to do afterwards."

. . .

They sat in the living room, covered in knitted blankets, and Val held Janice as the storm resumed and lashed the roof with a fresh downpour. Janice laced their fingers together and rested her temple against Val's shoulder, and they stared at the bookshelf where they tucked all the unread books Janice brought back from scavenging runs. "There's a lot of Agatha Christie," Val said.

"She wrote a lot of books, and they liked to keep her in print."

"I've never read one," Val said. "How'd we end up with seven books?"

"Seven I haven't read," Janice said. "There's more in the other room. She's a good read. Cosy, even with all the murders. I needed peace, I think. But I'm running out of books I haven't read. The Parker Pyne stories aren't Christie's best, at all, but I haven't read them yet."

Val stroked Janice's arm, and Janice shivered.

"The storm is picking up," Janice said. "I should go get some sleep, in case they need me."

Val rested a hand against Janice's hip. "I could go. They need more people."

"Jan—"

"It's not right to ask you to go back out so soon."

"Tonight's not the night to start volunteering."

"I can handle myself," Val said. "I know what to do."

The hand on Janice's hip felt heavy, an anchor weighing her in place. She turned and kissed Val on the lips, but it felt hollow. Like watching somebody else fake passion using Janice's body.

"I know you can handle yourself," Janice said. She removed Val's hand and got up, walked over to the window. Red lightning and dark clouds, the rain's crimson splatter. Janice could make out Val's concerned expression in the reflection in the window. Val rose and stood behind her, an arms-length back and to the left. Janice shifted her focus back to the scrub, wondered if she could see movement in the shadows or her brain just wanted to see the dead there and give her something to focus on.

"I'm going to turn in," Janice said. "You coming?"

"I'll wash up first. It's been a long day," Val said.

Janice stayed at the window a while longer, listening to the sluice and squeeze of Val cleaning with the sponge. The rain beat against the corrugated iron roof, growing louder as the storm picked up speed. Janice sighed and grabbed the window sill, held it in both hands. Out past the fence line, past the road, the gum trees swayed in the wind. The darkness and the storm would hide any dead approaching. Janice's shoulder's itched and she closed both eyes, focused on drawing in a slow, deep breath and exhaling it out again.

The militia would be out on patrol now, keeping watch on the slopes the dead could climb. Checking the streets to see if anyone passed away behind the defensive lines, reanimated by the downpour and set free to wander the mountaintop. Janice double checked all the locks and bars, then retreated to the bedroom. She shucked off her shorts and threadbare shirt, crawling into bed.

Val's book sat on the bedside table, one page dogeared. A battered *Two Towers* paperback, the pages yellowing and worn along the edges. Janice thought it might disintegrate if Val turned the page too aggressively, but Val had read two-thirds without incident. Janice turned on the solar lamp and positioned it over the book, closed the curtains, and crawled into bed. In the bathroom, Val sang as she finished washing, voice soft and hard to discern against the rain's rattle. Janice curled up beneath the covers, knees pulled to her chest.

She might feel better if she cried, but Janice couldn't force the tears. Sleep, then. She needed the sleep.

Val's song came to a halt. The water disappeared down a

drain with a gurgle.

Janice curled tight and listened to the rain, praying it would stop.

Val returned the basin to the counter and towelled off, biting her lower lip. She walked naked to the bedroom, skin dimpling with the cool. Whenever the rains came in force, they sucked the moisture from the air, turned the day's sweaty fugue into the low chill hinting at coming winter. She pulled pyjamas from the top drawer; a light t-shirt, and some drawstring shorts from the days before they scavenged everything. The t-shirt pink, the shorts purple. Val held them up in the lamplight, tried to look at Janice. Her wife lay still, her breathing slow.

"Do you remember the trip to Adelaide?" Val said. "We packed for the cold, but it's in the middle of the desert. You bought these at the Target on Rundle."

Janice replied with a cold look, then turned away.

Val went around to Janice's side of the bed. She knelt and took Janice's right hand, rubbed a thumb over the long fingers. "I know it's hard," she said. "Out there."

Janice didn't answer.

"I promise I can do my part," Val said. She risked a light stroke of Janice's temple, tangled fingers in her hair. "If they need someone, I'll go. I'll hold the line."

"If they need someone, maybe," Janice said.

"When will we know?"

Janice shrugged. "Deke'll send someone by if they need us. No need to go if we don't hear nothing."

"Good," Val said. "That's good. If we don't hear, I'll make a big breakfast. Fortify us for the day. If they call, we can go out together, maybe. Double the eyes, double the safety."

Janice pursed her lips and swallowed. She cupped one hand against the back of Val's head and leant over the bed to kiss her.

"If you're up for it, we can talk it over. After the rains," she said. "Right now, we should be sleeping."

Val nodded and released Janice's hand. She retreated and snuggled beneath the blankets. Her book sat on the bedside table, the solar lamp charged and ready to provide dim light if she wanted to read. It would mean going back, reviewing the last few pages. Nothing she read this afternoon had stuck, washed away by the constant fretting about what might happen if Janice didn't come home.

Val picked the book up and thumbed through the pages. She put it down again and turned out the light.

"I'm thinking it's time we relocated," Val said. "We're too close to the coast, out here. There's too many storms rolling in."

Janice went still at the idea. She pretended to be a big red, sniffing the air like he'd just caught a whiff of a hunter on the breeze, waiting for a sign he should bound off or turn around and fight. Val held her tongue, letting the silence stretch. Long, empty seconds.

But nothing hovered in that state of alert, poised for danger, indefinitely. Janice broke first, and said, "I like it here."

Val rolled on her side, laid one hand against Janice's cheek. "We've been here forever," she said. "We've been here since before the rains, and I wanted to leave back then. We should have gone home to Victoria, at some point. Lived near my parents and my sister."

"You think Melbourne's different from here?"

"I think everywhere's different from here," Val said. "Still dangerous. It's always dangerous, now. Doesn't mean we shouldn't leave, see what else is out there."

"Inland," Janice said. "Away from the storms."

"Seems like the smart call."

Janice stroked three fingers along Val's arm. Moved up

and cleared the strands of hair that fell across Val's face. Still so goddamned beautiful, like the night they met. Janice exhaled a cautious breath. "Doesn't strike me as the right call. Folks may not take to strangers showing up, now. Might not want us be part of their town."

Val tensed up, ready to argue, and Janice placed a finger against her lips. "But if it's what you want..."

Val's face lit up once the words registered, and she squirmed closer to hug Janice tight. They lay there, face to face. Janice slid her hand down Val's ribs, settled it over her butt. They kissed, and for a moment the old passion flared between them, furious and desperate. Janice bunched Val's dressing gown in a fist, pulled at it and moved one bare leg against her wife's exposed calf.

After, they lay together, limbs tangled, Val's head resting against Janice's chest. They listened to the howling wind and rain's steady tap overhead. Janice grappled with the logistics around moving on, packing up their gear and getting it across the empty spaces between the remaining towns. She tried to figure where they'd get the petrol, how they'd stay safe while on the road.

Val said, "you're thinking on it, aren't you?"

Janice traced a fingertip across Val's exposed shoulder and didn't give an answer.

"It's okay if we don't go," Val said. "I'd just like to consider it, yeah? I'd like to know it's an option?"

"Yeah."

"I know it wouldn't be your choice..."

"It's not that," Janice said. "It's really not."

But she couldn't say what it was.

Janice woke with the crack of thunder overhead, the rain hammering at the rooftop like a creature trying to beat its way in. Val's warmth still draped across her chest, heavy now Val had fallen asleep. Janice twisted, trying to get comfortable. The pressure felt oppressive, and she squirmed free. Turning on her side helped a little, but Janice couldn't find a comfortable way to lie. Val scooched close, breath hot on Janice's neck.

She tried to distract herself with Agatha Christie, trying to figure how the writer would spin a tale amid all this. They had the isolated houses, check. Small groups pushed to the limit. All they needed was a murder and a gentile detective, an outsider to make things right. Janice tried to remember the detectives she'd seen on TV. Little old ladies, or moustached Englishmen pretending they were Belgian. A redhead? She remembered a show with a redhead.

Thunder and lightning clashed outside, the strike close to the fence line. Janice blinked away the red spots, heart clattering as though it might shake free of its muscle and sinew moorings. Val slept comfortably, dead to the world. Janice focused on breathing in and out. 'Dead to the world' felt ominous now, all the years after the rain's first started.

Janice counted, six in and seven out. Bumped it up with each subsequent breath. The rain sluiced against the house, staining the windows crimson. Her pulse rate dropped to normal. Val murmured something in her sleep, twisted the blanket in her grip.

Not quite dead to the world, then.

Janice twisted free of the bed and crept over to the window. The darkness and the rain dropped visibility down to a few meters, the racket on the roof eliminating any chance they'd hear the dead approach if they got close to the house. Janice rubbed a palm against the window, clearing the glass. It didn't help. She couldn't see the fences, let alone the scrub beyond. The storm had shrunk their world down to the house. A wooden box, four bedrooms, a wide veranda. Corrugated iron rang like a thousand gongs as the storm picked up speed. Janice listened to the downpour, the nuances amid the cacophony. Water on steel, sloshing over the gutters and spilling in crimson sheets and hitting the ground with a guillotine's hiss. The creaking house shifting on its stumps, trying to settle amid the buffeting winds. The ground outside growing softer, muddier.

Thunder boomed again. A lightning strike flared across the sky, illuminating the landscape. Janice shielded her eyes with an arm, blinked away the spots. Were the deaders over in the field, shambling towards the house? She crouched and waited, not even breathing. Praying for another lightning strike, ears straining to catch the faintest sound that didn't belong to the storm.

No way to be sure, not amid all the noise. Janice went to the hallway and checked the guns. Collected the shotgun and spare shells, brought both back to the bed. She sat on the foot, facing the window. Leaned over and stroked Val's leg.

Better safe than sorry. "Val, wake up," she murmured.

But Val only pulled her leg away and twisted onto her side, eyes screwing tight. Val could sleep through anything, they'd joked, way back in the old days.

Janice levered a shell into the shotgun, her fingers shaking with the effort. "Babe, there's something out there," she said. "I think they're at the fence."

OUR SURVIVAL AND OTHER MYSTERIES

We all have stories, these days. Things that nailed shut the coffin on how things used to be, that made it clear the dead and the rain changed it all, and we weren't going back to normal. Riding past the abandoned Micky Ds you took your first date at age thirteen. Loading a shotgun after putting down the corpse of someone you loved. The first time you rolled over and reached for a gun, instead of the banger cell phone you've been coaxing through the past few years.

Me, I went to my Mother's house a little after midnight. The dead broke the lines at the top of my street, swarmed the neighborhood while I worked the late shift. I figured mum could spot me for a week, let me crash out on her couch. Buy myself a few days away from the trouble, putting a mask on around the shelter while Hadlee and I tamped down on our urge to argue. But when I got there, all the lights were on. The front door hung open, swinging in the breeze. I thought the worst, because you do these days. Crept in with a Smith & Wesson clenched in a tight grip. I found mum necking another woman, making out on the cracked leather couch she'd bought with dad on their thirtieth anniversary.

And yeah, you know. It happens. I hightailed it out of there.

My mother turns sixty-three this year. She'd been active in the militia for a while, riding shotgun with the black widow squad, hardest of the hard. Old broads who offed their spouses when the time came and it was necessary. Used to think that meant all the dead were men, but that's a bad habit from the old days. Nothing works like it did, before the dead. Adapt or die, like mum always said. The world changed when my father died, and again when he came back.

We ain't special, me or mum. Everybody's seen some shit these days. And things are better, for everyone, but at the moment, her girlfriend knocked me sideways. I didn't take it well.

Thing is, Hadlee was cheating on me, getting together with one of the buzz-saws the militia sent out to mop up the dead. A short, hard bloke they'd dubbed The Chin, who she'd met at the local AA earlier that year. Like most buzz-saws, The Chin was crazy. Hadlee was into that.

The Chin's real name was Sam. Samuel Morrison. He'd lost his left hand to the dead a while back, got bit defending a wheat field and lopped it off to prevent the infection spreading. Lots of folks figured it tainted him, but he showed no signs of infection. Only sign he'd been through anything was the drinking and his lopsided walk, weighted down by the DeWalt chainsaw he'd fixed to stump once it healed. Whole thing only weighed a couple of kilograms, but it turned out that's enough to affect your balance. Sure as hell did the job for my wife.

The Chin had been married once, as well. Lost his wife to the dead in the first uprising, the same one that took out my dad. He was a little guy, short but well-built. Chin you could use to break granite, and he still shaved every morning instead of letting the beard grow long. I hated the guy back then, you know? Don't know how I feel about him now. He's been good to my daughter, I'll give him that.

Good to Hadlee, too, when he's home. 'Specially given he's not so crazy now. But my daughter, Eleanor, she says Hadlee worries. Every time The Chin is out on patrol, she's convinced he's not coming back.

"It weighs on her," Eleanor says. "I keep worrying she'll, you know…"

Eleanor mimes taking a hit from a flask, but flasks were never Hadlee's thing.

"Don't worry," I tell her. "It's not like it was."

"But it could be," Eleanor says. "Couldn't it?"

In his crazier days, The Chin went out on patrol three or four times a week. He bunked in the guard house out by the south edge of the wheat fields. Crazy bastard constructed his own personal gauntlet for the dead to run through. Spiked pits. Moats and choke-points. One or two homemade landmines. Once or twice, he'd shown up at the first aid tent bleeding from his own defenses. He'd get drunk and forget the safe route through, or the damn chainsaw tipped him over once the whiskey affected his balance.

In the early days of their affair, before she'd admitted she wanted him physically, Hadlee claimed The Chin had been a soldier in the days before the dead. I've seen his medical records; he'd been a reservist: one weekend a month, two weeks a year of service. It wasn't nothing, but it wasn't something either. Reserve hadn't been a big deal for decades. Regular army didn't know what to do with 'em. Only came in handy once the dead rose, and some folks rose to the occasion with 'em.

But I'll give The Chin this: he survived when other folks didn't. Against all fucking odds, he came back from patrol.

Survived the accidents around his guard house with scrapes and cuts and bruises. Survived the drinking, just like Hadlee, and that ain't nothing, don't you think?

The first thing you admit in meetings is your lack of power over your addiction, that your life has become unmanageable. First time I went after the dead rose… well, there's plenty of practice now. We don't control shit no more.

On a bad night, weeks before things with The Chin got started, Hadlee lit into me about my choices. "You react," she said. "You just wait and patch up the people who get hurt. Everyone else is taking steps, and you're mopping up once they're done. If you'd just…"

She never finished the thought. I never followed up. She's joined the meetings, and then the militia. Needed something to fill the nights now she'd stopped draining bottles of Merlot on our back deck. She'd go out three or four times a week, while I stayed home and drank our stash of whiskey.

Ostensibly, keeping Eleanor safe, in case the dead broke in.

We tell ourselves comforting stories about how and why we do things. Hadlee didn't feel like she'd betrayed me; she simply accepted the least awful choice in an impossible situation.

It started with a meeting and became a routine. Four times a week, Hadlee accepted her lack of power and shared stories with the group, then moved over to C&C to give a few hours to the militia. Idle hands in need of occupation reached for familiar sources of comfort, so it's no surprise half her meeting did the same thing.

The Chin only sported one idle hand, but he needed more occupation than most. The militia made them a team, the buzz-saw and the sharpshooter assigned to get him home safe. Carving through the dead with his DeWalt and her .303.

I can't blame her for falling for him. I can't blame her for walking away from me.

All this happened five or six years back, before we'd adjusted to the dead a bit. You may remember those days were crazy, compared to the way things settled in recent years. I say the thing with my mother started it, but that was just a trigger. A moment I realized nothing could stay the same, and all my comforting stories were only so much fiction.

When I fled my mother's house, trying to forget the sight of her necking her new girlfriend, I knew I couldn't face Hadlee without doing something stupid. So I walked around for a few hours, checking the perimeter. Making sure all the lines were holding, patching up the militia members who'd got injured holding back the dead. It wasn't like it'd been in days before: I'd grown used to the pop of guns in the night, the hurried call of the militia filling gaps as the dead advanced down suburban streets. The sea of unfamiliar stars, all of them emerging from the cloak of night once the light pollution eased.

I thought: We'd done good, as a species, really. Held the dead at bay more often than not. The detritus of the old world lingered, reminding us all it wasn't so bad. We still encountered abandoned skateboards and bikes in kid's front yards; the scent of eucalyptus in the air; volunteers serving soup to the volunteers coming off shift, trading smiles and jokes and comfort.

But I couldn't walk forever, and exhaustion pushed me into the shelter where wife and daughter waited. Hadlee, awake and fretting, or hoping she could sidestep the choice she didn't want to make. Eleanor, sleeping fitfully beneath the scratch, donated sheets washed with too much bleach.

"You look hungry," Hadlee said, first thing. Easier than picking a fight. "Sit down. I'll rustle up some food."

I sat, surrounded by friends and neighbors, all of us packed into emergency cots arranged in rows across the warehouse. Hadlee reappeared with a bowl of tomato soup and two dry slices of toast. I ate while Hadlee sat on the other cot, stroking Eleanor's hair.

"We were worried," Hadlee said. She kept her voice low and soft.

"Dead blocked the road back from the clinic," I said. "Had to find an alternate route."

"We still worried." Hadlee took an interest in the green exit sign glowing on the far side of the shelter. "You want a cup of tea? I should have brought you a cup of tea, yeah?"

I didn't want a tea, and said so. She went anyway, taking the excuse. I waited until she was on the far side of the room before I fished the silver flask out of my pocket and drained the whiskey.

Our stash of booze was running out. Eventually, I'd need to salvage more, and that meant going past the boundary.

I told this story to my daughter, once, not long after she'd turned nineteen. Carefully edited, because Hadlee's still her mum. Because The Chin is the father figure she saw five days out of every seven. Eleanor listened, eyes hooded, fingers curled around a mug of tea. She focused on details I'd never expected.

"You took your first date to Micky Ds?" she said. "No wonder mum left your ass."

"It wasn't like she was my date," I said. "I was thirteen. It was the eighties."

Eleanor snorted, like that meant something to her. Like the dead hadn't bifurcated her adult life into two epochs: before and after they rose.

. . .

I tell myself Hadlee loved The Chin, in her way, otherwise it wouldn't have lasted.

The Chin lost his hand at thirty-three, and he already loved the chainsaw more than he'd loved any living thing. Some folks, they found themselves when the dead rose, discovered a wellspring of resilience they hadn't needed prior. I don't blame him for the drinking, you know? To realize how much he loved carving through the dead, to reconcile that kind of violence with the person he'd been before, that wasn't a simple thing. He'd been an army reservist, sure, but he'd sold real estate the other weeks of the year. Hadlee had programed spreadsheets for a living. I'd delivered vaccinations and gave kids lollipops after their check-ups.

We are none of us who we used to be. We'd ceded control over our lives, had adapted and learned to live with the dead, clawed back what normalcy we could.

The Chin told Eleanor he used to sell three-bedrooms up on Windsor hill. Ordinarily, everyday houses who tripled in value as the years went by, six-figure homes turning into seven figures as the world changed around them. "Funny thing," he said, "they're worth nothing now. Council just assigns them."

We are none of us who we used to be.

"He's not a dangerous man," Hadlee told me once. "He doesn't take the chances people think. He thinks it through. He understands the risk, weighs against what the rest of his team really needs."

I told Hadlee I'd believe that. She wouldn't blow our lives up for a reckless nobody.

. . .

My father died fighting at fifty-six, in the first three days of the rains and the dead. We'd watched the news with horror, seen the footage, stayed put. He armed himself with an axe and a shovel from the garden shed, filled the bathtub and every container we could with fresh water from the tap. "Everything will be fine in a bit," he said. "Someone will do something if it's serious."

We ate ham and cheese sandwiches for dinner, using up what we could from the fridge. After dinner, my dad stood vigil with the axe. He drank a six-pack of VB, watching the empty streets. He followed it with a half-bottle of wine, his voice growing flossy when he came in to report, assuring us it would be okay.

My mother warned him to stop, but my father had long since inured himself to any attempt to curb his drinking. When the dead came, he strode down the stairs with the axe, belligerent and eager to split some skulls. My mother locked him out there. She locked us in the small room beneath the stairs.

Made one attempt to venture out and assure the coast was clear, only to discover my father's corpse on the move. Hunting for fresh meat.

She caved his skull in with a shovel and locked us down again. We stayed put for three days and six hours, when the army swept our suburb for survivors and checked us both for signs of infection.

My mother, at age sixty-three, got an undercut and her first tattoo. She's thinner than she'd been while married to my father, sheathed in lean muscle and scar tissue. Dangerous in a way I'd never expected my mother to be. On the night I told her Hadlee and I were done, she'd disassembled her 9mm and cleaned each part at the dinner table. Upon my arrival, she took one look at my face and set the job aside.

She'd sat me down on the leather couch with a cup of tea. Listened to my story, the breakdown of cause and effect.

"You made the right choice," she said, but it wasn't my choice. Not really.

I told Hadlee I could change on the night she left me. "I'll go to meetings again," I said. "I'll pull it together, I promise."

She said, "It's not about meetings, honey."

Then she hugged me and held me tight for a while, as if it might be the last thing we did.

THE MIRACLE MAN EATS

I'm sitting on Langston's couch with a cigarette between two fingers and a half-eaten slice of three-cheese pizza on a plate in my lap. Langston fusses in the kitchen, making us both a cup of tea. He's worried, and he's right to be worried. I'm almost done, he tells me. Then you can lay it all out, yeah?

He returns with a cup of rooibos. The last time I drank rooibos tea, I broke out in hives. Langston knows this, but he's forgotten. Tell me what happened, he says.

So, I do, and this is what I tell him.

We're in the quiet lull before the evening shift when Vince seats the Miracle Man at the corner station. There's two of us on, me and Laura, and it's her station, but she doesn't want to get close. Vince grumbles at her, then grumbles at me, then tells me I've got to serve him.

Fine.

The Miracle Man, back from the dead. Stitched together from seven different cadavers, but there's a living brain behind it all I'd seen him before, on YouTube, on TikTok, but it wasn't a thing like seeing him in real life. Cameras focus on the obvious things, pull your eyes to the black seams where they stitched him together, but you loose track of that when you're up close in the real world, you know? What stays with you is the way he lists to one side, the sallow cheeks, the absence of a smell your brain expects but can't place. Like walking the meat aisle at the supermarket, surrounded by all that bloody flesh, but you're sealed away from the horror of it by bright lights and a thin veneer of plastic wrap.

What stays with you is the fact he's walking around without a gun, because the dead ain't going to eat him, not given how they sourced the parts to bring him back. God, Lang, can you imagine that? Not having to drill? Not having to check for bites? Not having to check you've reloaded every time you leave the house? It seems like heaven, don't it, until you figure out the cost.

Still, none of that's on him, you know? I treat him like any other customer. Hey sir, how you doing today, all of that. I give him a menu and run through the specials and promise the lamb and vege gratin is better than it sounds. I ask him if he's ready to order.

Sure, he says. I'm ready.

Hasn't even glanced at the menu yet, but that's no skin off my nose. I ask him what he's after and he hems and haws a moment, clearing his throat. I think I'll start with the gratin, he says. A toasted chicken and avocado sandwich, he says. With a side of fries. A slice of the apple pie with ice cream, and a latte with skim milk.

Regular or large, I ask him.

Large, he says. Hot as you can make it. I like things hot, these days.

Chef makes a killer chili, I tell him. Fills you up real good, tastes like a slice of heaven. Spicy, too, if you like the other kind of heat.

Fine, the Miracle Man says. I'll have that too. And he hands me back the menu, still not giving it a glance, just watching the whole diner like we're a snack-packs walking around, like, and I can tell we're all just nervous, yeah?

Everybody's thinking about him, and how he got built, and what they'll do if his miracle ain't so miraculous. If he's just another deader, ready to go out and chomp some brains.

But my job ain't to fret about that none. I just take his order to he kitchen, turn it over to Bowie. He takes it, and he puts two-and-two together, and he pulls that face he gets when he's gearing up to argue, but I cut him off. Just don't, I say. We can't make a scene about this.

Like hell we can't, Bowie says, but he leaves it at that, thank heavens. He gets to work and starts the grill and gives me the space to go refill the coffees of the old couple in the last booth, and all the while Laura's over in the corner, bitching to Vince about all this. It ain't fair we got to serve him, she says. It ain't right that thing is here.

Only she says it loud, not really a private conversation. A little performance we're all meant to hear.

You ain't serving him, Vince says. Megan's covering the table, so shut your lip.

I aint working with in the same room as a deader, Laura says. I'm walking out, right damn now, if you make me.

Don't let the door hit you on the ass, Vince says, like it ain't no big deal if she goes.

Which is how I end up covering the whole damn floor, right before shit goes to hell.

I like to think I don't hold grudges. You know me, Lang, I let folks be who they gotta be. I don't blame Laura for walking off, and I don't blame Vince for pushing her into it. She's got a right to say her piece, and he's got a business to run, you know? But it don't change the fact that I'm in the weeds now, and I blame her more than I blame him. The next ten minutes, I'm running like a crazy person, and Vince pitches in, but you know how Vince is, yeah? Never quite the savior he thinks he is, on those moments he deigns to work the floor instead of jawing with the regulars while he makes their coffee.

Things go wrong and nobody gets their food on time, you know? But you do your best, and you smile at folks, and you play it like it's no big deal, and most folks can be understanding about it. Most folks, but not everyone, and the whole time the Miracle Man's food is sitting underneath he warmer, I'm getting worried about how he's going to play it. Getting worried about him getting hungry, like he might snap and eat us all.

He's been waiting fifteen minutes for his coffee because Vince isn't working the machine, and his tagine is waiting for pick-up. So I haul ass and get him the coffee first, offer up my apologies. I'm so sorry about all this, sir. Busiest part of the evening and all that.

Fine, he says. It's fine, and his lips peel away from his teeth in a way that's probably meant to be a smile. I can tell you're busy, he says. I'm so sorry if I'm part of that.

Not at all, I tell him, then I go get the first course of his meal. When I get back with the tagine I notice he isn't drinking his coffee at all. Just stirring in sugar, cupping the mug in one hand, soaking in its warmth. I deliver the tagine and he smiles at me again, and a part of me wants to shrivel up and scream to block the memory out. He doesn't reach for a knife and fork, doesn't try to season the tagine. Just pulls the plate a little closer, lets it cool at his elbow.

We're busy as hell, but I still notice. I still drop buy and do the whole thing: everything going okay, sir? Your sandwich will be out in a second.

It's fine, he says. It's great. Appetite takes a bit to kick in these days, but when it does, I'm ravenous.

Well, when it happens, you're covered, I say. Chef makes a kick-ass tagine.

It smells delicious, he says, which is more polite than he ought to be. Bowie's learned to cook on a fry grill at Mickie Ds, scored a job as our cook because we needed someone and our last chef got drunk and got himself eaten trying to walk home from the Valley. Vince needed someone and Bowie was the best choice we had, and he's okay, but sometimes I'm telling the customers what ought to be true instead of what is, you know?

But the Miracle Man, he seems real happy. He puts his nose over the tagine and breathes in deep and smiles his lopsided smile. He arranges his napkin and moves his cutlery around and makes a show of really loving the meal seated before him.

And he doesn't take a bite, Lang. Just moves it around the plate some. He doesn't take a bite and he's still got four courses to go, and I start to get worried.

The crowd's thinned out some by the time his chicken sandwich is ready, and I bring it over with another coffee. Gift from the manager, I say. For being patient. Been one hell of a day.

Thank you, he says. I appreciate that. He says, this tagine is rather specular. My compliments to the chef.

I'll pass that on, I tell him.

Please do, he says. I mean it. I don't often choose to eat out like this, you know? Not since…

He waved a hand at his face, and his meaning is clear. Not since they rebuilt him out of the dead, brought him back to life.

I'm real sorry about Laura, I tell him. The other waitress, before. She ain't got no right to make a scene like that.

It's fine, he says. It happens.

It's gotta suck, I tell him.

I make the best of things, he says. They say a positive outlook helps.

Still, I say, it wasn't professional. How was your tagine?

Great, he says. It's all fine.

My eyes fall on the plate. It still contains the same quantity of tagine, just churned up by a knife and fork.

You sure?

Then he does this little glance, like most folks do when they're embarrassed, but I don't think his body can blush no more. It just keeps on keeping on.

Thing is, he says, I don't eat much anymore.

Ordered a lot of food for a man who doesn't eat, I tell him.

I still get hungry, he says. My stomach doesn't work right, but I used to love eating. I like to sit and remember and smell the food, feel the warmth of things straight from the oven. Reminds me I used to be somebody else.

His laugh sounds like an emptying drain. He spears the sandwich with a fork, cuts it open and watches the cheese stretch. Playing with food like a little kid.

I used to be lots of somebodies, he says, a private joke as he makes the best of things.

I go off to take care of my other tables. Deliver chili to an older couple, down in the corner. Take care of the two kids on their first date, snacking on fries while they drink chocolate milkshakes. There's a few lawyers floating around, guns in shoulder holsters. Extra ammunition packed into their briefcases. They keep ordering bottles of red wine, a celebration of something. One cracks a joke about representing the Miracle Man if he sues the restaurant on account of Laura's behavior. That one's ont funny either, but the other lawyers laugh along with him. I don't like the lawyers much. They're too loud, too aggressive, too drunk.

The Miracle Man's chili order is up, so I hustle over to grab it. Bowie leaves the grill to put his two cents in, making noise about working hard on that food. Why's this guy disrespecting him by letting it sit there, not even bothering to taste. I tell Bowie about the Miracle Man's stomach, how he's just here to get a whiff of things, and Bowie grumps and stomps back to the grill and rumbles about how it ain't right. Then Vince intercepts me after I grab the order. Pulls me close and keeps his voice low, tells me to get the Miracle Man outta there. Fast as you can, he says. He's making folks nervous around here. He's not eating the food he ordered.

I think about telling Vince to go fuck himself, but what good does that do anyone. Do what I can, I tell him.

And I take the Miracle Man his chili.

Right away, I can tell he's not in good shape. Sitting over a cut-up sandwich, the whole thing rendered down to bite-sized chunks nobody will ever eat. The Miracle Man is listing to his left, his face drawn tight like he's in pain. Eyes tracking movement throughout the café with a predator's focus. We all know that look, these days, only the Miracle Man's not sweating. He's not keeling over, about to die. His eyes aren't changing colour. Still, it's making folks right nervous. All that time we spend drilling safety protocols, all that talk about acting fast instead of waiting for folks to turn. All those adds reminding us we're in this together, they do their job. I'm itching to draw my .45 and plug him between the eyes, but I don't. He's not a dead man. He's a walking miracle. He's the silver lining of all this shit, you know?

Steam curls off the bowl of child. The meat and beans are piping hot, bowl still warm from the oven. I swallow my fear and say, want me to clear some of these plates?

Please, he says. Then he says, you'll have to excuse me a moment. I'm not feeling like myself.

I don't see how you could, I say. Must be hard, being a miracle.

It doesn't feel like much of a miracle, he says.

He arranges his napkin. He picks up a spoon. He stirs the chili, but it doesn't feel natural. He's stiff. Every move requires thought, nothing automatic. It's work to tell the fingers to grip, the wrist to flex and stir.

It'll pass soon, he says. Please don't be alarmed.

I'm not alarmed, I say. It's a lie, but I say it.

It's not enough, so I add: We're all cool with you being here, honest.

Right. He looks at me, that predator look. He doesn't look away.

Listen, I say, do you need us to call someone? Is there something we can do?

Meat, he says.

Meat?

Raw meat, he says. A steak, raw. Not bloody, raw. Only thing I can still digest. Only thing that'll help. I don't want—

And he closes his eyes here. Closes his eyes and looks away, like he hates saying this out loud. I don't want to do this in public, he says. If you bring it out in a to-go bag, I can take it to the bathroom.

I write down the order like it's no big deal. Okay, I tell him. One steak, raw meat. I'm sure I can make that happen.

More, he says. More than one, if you can.

No problem, I say, and I bail on him. I go back to the kitchen and tell Bowie to empty the freezer. I go tell Vince so he can figure out what we're charging the Miracle Man for all this. One by one, the café empties out. The young couple finish their date, abruptly. The lawyers move on to the bar across the street. Vince frets about the Miracle Man, wonders if we should call in a threat, but I figure we should trust the guy.

Langston fumbles for one of my cigarettes. He puts his two cents in. Jesus, he says. Weren't you scared?

For sure, I say. But that don't mean shit. He knew more about being the Miracle Man than I did, know what I'm saying? If he says raw meat will make things better, why in hell should I doubt him?

I would have shot him, Langston says.

Well, you weren't there, I say. Also, I can't drink this tea. Rooibos tea gives me hives. I'm allergic or something. You know that, Lang. I've told you before.

Shit, he says. Sorry.

•   •   •

Langston heads for the kitchen, and I think about the parts of the story I'm never going to tell him. The part where Vince frets the whole time about my safety, asking to cover my table. The part when I got that feeling that wasn't fear, exactly. More excitement at knowing fear waited in the wings, ready to swoop in.

The relief when the Miracle Man left, and I'd done it. We'd done it. The heady feeling that we'd survived it together, the diner working as a team.

The part where Vince pulled me aside and we kissed like haven't kissed in years. I don't tell Langston about any of that.

He brings the earl gray, and I tell him the other rest.

The café's almost empty when I start bringing out the meat. We kick off with three steaks, tucked away in a doggie bag. The Miracle Man limps into the bathroom and stays there for three minutes. He reappears with colour on his lips, settles back into the table. I'd like to enjoy my chili now, he says. Bring out the next round of meat before the pie, please.

The next round of meat is a tray of raw mince, and it goes down as fast as the steaks do. The Miracle Man, he perks up with the meat in his belly. He moves a little smother, doesn't stare at the other customers when they finish up and visit the counter to pay for their meal. I bring out his pie with a little ice cream on the size. I put the plate in front of him.

Thank you, he says.

No problem, I say. You're very welcome.

It isn't always like this, he says. Most days, I'm out in public, and it's just like it was before.

I believe you, I say. It must be hard.

It is, he says. But it's hard for everyone, these days. It's been hard since this all began.

Ain't that the truth, I tell him. Still, you bear it well.

You find your moments where it still feels good, he says. And, mostly, you lie to yourself, you know? You tell yourself it's fine, no matter what.

Then he picks up the spoon and breaks the pie crust. He scoops out the filling and dips it in the ice cream, studies the spoonful with a critical eye. He says, will you eat this for me? I can't eat it, but it would be nice to see someone enjoy it.

Vince is watching me like a hawk, waiting for things to go sideways. Bowie is over in the kitchen, cleaning the girl so we can shut up for the night the moment the Miracle Man leaves. Neither of them is happy to be there, now. Vince won't approve of me taking food from him.

But hell, this guy's life is bad enough. It's something I can do for him. So, I take the spoon and I eat the pie. It's not great, but it's good. It'll do. It's a treat, you know? I chew it up and I swallow, and I give him a smile.

What happens next? Langston says. How did things go wrong?

It didn't, I say. He finishes up and pays for his meal. He leaves a big team as he leaves. People leave the café all the time. I clear his plates and wipe the tables down and Vince says something about it being a hard day. Then Vince loads up the shotgun and gives me the keys, and we do the long drive to his place instead of staying the night at mine. There's not too many deaders out, not this time of year, but he takes a shot at any that wander too close, even when they're not a threat.

Vince likes to shoot deaders, when he's pissed. I'm not even sure why he's angry.

We make it home just before midnight. It's been a long day. Long as hell. Vince makes noise about cooking us something for dinner, but in the end we reheat yesterday's ravioli and curl up in front of the TV. After we eat, Vince gets up and checks the perimeter. Wants to make sure the fence is intact, wants to make sure all the guns are loaded. He's keyed up, ready to pick a fight. And I'm not there, so I go take a shower. I make it hot, hot as I can bear to make it, and scrub my skin clean and pink. I don't tell Langston about what comes after, about Vince and I having sex again, first time in an age. About feeling alive with Vince's hands on me, and feeling alive when I'm touching him.

I don't tell him how it felt like the old days, before, and it's turned into something colder now. Something angrier than it was, and we talk even less.

I don't know how to tell Langston any of that, so I'm telling him the other stuff instead.

Okay, Langston says, and he lights another cigarette. Just making sure I've got this clear. Nobody tried to eat you, yeah? It was just one of those asshole days, busy, and you felt a bit weird?

Yeah, I say. I guess that's mostly it.

Baby, he says, you're one strange bird. Then he says, I'm sorry about your tea. I swear I'll remember, this time, okay?

He reaches out and strokes me arm a little. Makes it clear we are done with this part of the evening, the part where he listens and pretends to care about the minutia of my life.

I say thing the right things, because I know them by heart by now. It's okay, I say. It happens. It's fine.

It's not fine, he says. I love you, baby.

Langston believes he's a good guy. Believes he's good for me. Maybe, at one point, that was true. We go to bed, after. It's perfectly okay. Nothing like what I had with Vince, that night. Nothing like what it had been in the past. I'm feeling stuck, but I can't say that to Langston.

It's not like he'd hear me, anyway.

Outside, it's cold. The first breath of winter on the wind. There's storm clouds gathering, red rain on the horizon. The promise of fresh dead rising up as it sweeps through.

I know this can't go on anymore, but maybe it can last until spring.

EVERYTHING MUST GO

Tillie parked her arse on the front step, twelve-gauge across her lap. She poured a whiskey and glared at the pile of stuff assembled on the front yard: the bedroom suite and bedside tables; the crates filled with Mark's old records; the kids board games from the front room, alongside the crates of mismatched Legos from three generations of Carmichaels. Everything which made her house a home, disgorged and arranged for public consumption. Tillie drank a slug of whiskey. It didn't help things much.

Their old couch hunched a meter and a half from the bed. Black leather, worn with age now, and sagging with the accumulated effort of holding so many of Tillie's family for so long. Mark's red folding table sat beside the couch, just as it did inside. Mark would unfold it to eat dinner in front of the TV, or use it to play solitaire when he wanted to clear his mind. The notion of selling the table hurt. It felt too much like losing him all over, and tears prickled Tillie's eyes.

She blinked them away and drank. Resolve. Adjusted the shotgun so she could sit comfortably.

The kitchen table was on the far side of the yard, chairs stacked in a heap beside it. Cutlery and crockery spread out across the tabletop so folks could get a real good look. Sterling silver, because Mark insisted. No point saving the good forks for company. A broken blender they'd stashed in the back of the cupboard because Mark insisted he could fix it, and never did.

There were signs out. Garage Sale. Everything must go.

Tillie wasn't expecting nobody, because why pay for other people's junk these days? Why show up in the wee hours to get a good bargain when whole suburbs were emptied of anything but the dead? The undead had no need for blenders or tables, for leftover toilet paper and bottles of good rye. You could just go out and take stuff.

Tillie drained her paper cup of whiskey. Poured herself another.

Wondered if she could just leave this, the detritus of their life together, if nobody showed up.

"Holy shit, a yard sale," Jacks said to Arthur.

Arthur wrinkled his nose. "A what?"

Jacks squeezed Arthur's hand and pointed down the block. Arthur squinted at the furniture arranged on the lawn. "What in hell is she doing?"

"Selling her things."

"To whom?" Arthur said.

"Whoever comes along. Lets take a closer look," Jacks said. She tugged on his arm, but Arthur didn't move.

"It might be a trap," he said.

"It's not a trap. We're in town. Militia's patrolling the fence," Jacks said.

"The dead are getting smarter. Everybody says so."

"Marty Dubois says so, and his dad's a MAGA idiot."

"So?"

"We're not in America, mate. Nothing to make great again here," Jacks said.

"I just don't think it's safe," Arthur said. "Getting up close in someone's yard like that, poking through their stuff."

"Let's go check it out," Jacks repeated. "If she's a deader, you can say 'I told you so' in a smug tone before we shoot her."

Arthur squinted and laid a hand on the revolver at his hip. They crossed the road, hand-in-hand. Walked the block to the cluttered lawn. Then they released their grip and began to rummage. Jacks pulled clothes out of boxes, running her fingers over fabrics worn soft by the years of effort. Arthur crouched beside an old record player, moving the turntable with his fingers, trying to gauge how it might work. Jacks picked up an old cricket bat and swung it, getting a feel for the weight.

Arthur crossed the yard, heading for the big Queen bed by the drive, and flopped his weight into the mattress. He spread his arms and stared at the blue sky, no hint of a cloud. "Jacks," he said. "Come try this."

Jacks crossed the yard to join him, weaving between detritus spread across the grass. The owner sat on the front step, pouring booze into a paper cup. Jacks met her glance and looked away. Drunk, probably. This early in the morning.

Arthur grabbed Jacks' wrist and pulled her onto the bed. He wrapped skinny arms around her and kissed her neck. The bed was firm and comfortable. Arthur's kisses were dry and papery—he wasn't drinking enough water.

"This isn't bad." Arthur lay back. Jacks nestled into his shoulder. They stared at the bright blue sky above. "This isn't bad at all," he said.

Jacks rubbed Arthur's chest. "The owner's watching us."

"What do we do if we want this?"

"We pay them."

"With what?"

Jacks scrunched her face and contemplated the question.

She had a faint notion of money, inherited from her parents. "You'll have to ask them. They're over on the stair."

Arthur lifted himself off the mattress and cleared his throat. "Excuse me?"

The owner raised her eyebrows.

"How much?" Arthur said.

"What are you offering?"

Barter, then. Arthur shared a look with Jacks. They didn't have much. They'd laid claim to an abandoned two-bedroom place down by the wall. Jacks placed two fingers together and raised her thumb, signalling an offer.

"We got ammo," Arthur said. "Nine millimetre."

"Ammo is good," the owner said. "I can always use ammunition."

"We can give you a half a box," Arthur said. "Twenty-five rounds. Bed will save us that much if we don't have to go beyond the wall."

Tillie poured another whiskey and weighed up the kid's offer. She didn't really need the bullets, but it wouldn't hurt to have them. All she really wanted was the bed gone, along with all the memories. A chance to restart. "I could let you have it for fifty rounds," she said. "You can get them here today?"

"Tomorrow."

"Today would be better. I'm leaving town."

The kid raised his finger and leant over his girl to confer. He straightened, affecting a smile. "We can do today."

"Great."

"You got a lot of nice stuff here," the kid said.

"Had," Tillie said. "It's all gotta go."

"You aren't getting many takers," the kid said.

Tillie knocked back the whiskey, draining half the cup. Picking up speed now instead of practicing restraint. "No," she said. "Not many."

"I'm Arthur," the kid said. "This is Jacks."

"Hello Arthur," Tillie said.

The girl—Jacks—poked her head up for the first time. "You got a name?"

"I'm Tillie. Tillie Carmichael."

Tillie waited, breath trapped behind her teeth, in case they recognised the name. News about Mark and the kids got around, but it hadn't reached Arthur and Jacks.

Jacks slid off the bed and surveyed the yard. "Don't see many yard sales these days, Tillie Werner."

"No."

"You doing okay?"

The question drew a pang of sorrow deep in Tillie's chest. "I'm leaving. I'm going to Tucson."

"Tucson in America?"

"That's the one."

Jacks whistled. "Long haul."

"My husband's family lived there."

"Your husband going with you?"

"No."

Jacks looked at Arthur. She screwed her face up, rubbed both hands against her jeans, searching for purchase. "Deaders, depression, or divorce?"

"Deaders," Tillie said.

"Damn," Jacks said. "I'm sorry."

"Me too," Arthur said.

Tillie set the shotgun aside. She stood and stretched her beck and stooped over to collect her paper cup. The empty bottle of scotch sat beside her gun on the step.

"I'm about to break the seal on a bottle of Johnny. You kids want a slug?"

The kids exchanged another glance.

"Sure," Arthur said.

Tillie gestured at the kitchen table. "Grab yourself a glass. I'll be back in a jiff."

.   .   .

There were no whiskey glasses on the table. There were thirteen coffee mugs: seven black, two white with astronauts printed on the side, one bearing a faded high school coat of arms, one bearing a shirtless cowboy with six-pack abs. The remaining two proclaimed the drinker "World's Best Dad", or promised "No Wucking Furries", and Jacks decided neither was the best choice. She selected an astronaut mug and handed Arthur the shirtless cowboy. They brought their mugs to the front steps and waited for Tillie's return.

Arthur sat on the low step and puffed his cheeks out. "I'm not sure that bed's worth a half-box."

"Close enough to," Jacks said.

"You think?"

"Way you shoot? We'd go through twenty-five just trying to hold off three or four deaders on a scavenger run."

"Fuck you," Arthur said.

Tillie returned with a fresh bottle of whiskey. She poured a slug into the cowboy mug and the astronaut mug. Poured a full paper cup of her own, filling it to the brim. She emptied it just as quickly, then went back for another round.

Jacks sipped her whiskey carefully. Arthur didn't touch his at all. Twilight crept up on them, and the solar lights in Tillie's yard lit up.

Tillie pulled the shotgun onto her lap. Jacks eyed the drunk woman's movements, wary of the barrel. She didn't think Tillie would shoot them, but drunk people did stupid things.

There were gunshots in the distance. Militia patrolling the fields the wall, protecting the food supply. Arthur carried his still-full scotch through the yard, eyeing an old pushbike.

Tillie winced at every gunshot, closed her eyes and turned her face away, shoulders bunched. Her face taut, although Jacks couldn't tell if it stemmed from anger, grief, or fear.

. . .

"How are you getting to Tucson?"

The young girl, Jacks, shifted her weight from left foot to right. She sipped her Whiskey from one of Mark's mugs, pretended she hadn't noticed the militia holding off the dead in the wheat fields outside town. Tillie wondered how old they were, Jacks and Arthur. Born before the rains, certainly, but they'd grown up in a world where the dead returned. They'd learned to shoot alongside their ABCs, knew some of their friends wouldn't survive to adulthood. They knew how to lose people.

Jacks raised her eyebrows, waiting. Tillie swallowed the knot in her throat, washed it down with a slug. "The Americans still run planes," she said. "My husband worked for their base up in Rocky. I'm road-tripping up there, and one of his friends is a pilot. He'll get me to the states."

Jacks finished her drink. Held out the mug for more. "You really think you'll find family out there? Word is, the American's caused this. They took the worst of it."

Tillie wanted to slap her. Instead, she poured a slug of whiskey into the ceramic cup. "I think it's a longshot, but it's better than staying here."

Jacks nodded once. "I get that," she said.

Tillie didn't believe her, but it was a nice thought. The young lost too much too early these days. They didn't remember what life used to be before the rains and the dead.

"I'm going to get out a board game," Tillie said. "There's dozens of them, in that trunk over there. I'll throw them in with the bed, if you want."

She poured another cup of whiskey. She didn't get off the stoop. "You guys want to play Carcassonne?"

Arthur looked up from the bike, frowning. "Carcassonne's a city in France."

"It's a game too," Tillie said.

Jacks considered her half-drunk whiskey. She assessed the way Arthur fussed with the bike, testing the chain and the tyres.

"I'll get it," she said.

She found the box of games over by the table, tucked away on a hardwood seat. There were familiar titles in the box—Monopoly, and Chinese Checkers—but she didn't recognise the names or artwork of the other games. She pulled the Monopoly free from the pile. "I played this as a kid," she said. "My mother loved it."

Tillie rolled her eyes. Arthur didn't look away from the bike. Jacks put the board game down and rummaged through the unfamiliar contents. The board game Tillie wanted to play was in a small box with yellow letters. The cover art featured a walled city, ancient stonework running between guard towers. Easily defensible. I could hold the dead off for months.

Arthur said, "how much for the bike?"

"Make me an offer," Tillie said.

Arthur screwed his face to one side. "Another six bullets?"

"I'll take it."

Jacks brought the game to the house steps, placed it beside Tillie.

"This was my daughters," Tillie said.

"I've never played."

"That's okay. I'll teach you."

"I'm going to get your bullets," Arthur said. "Can I take the bike? Cut down on the walk?"

Tillie shrugged at the question, busy sorting tiles and little blue men made of wood. There were rivers on the tiles, and lengths of walled city. Arthur took her distraction as acceptance and left, swinging a leg over the pushbike and cycling ino the distance.

Tillie poured Jacks another cup of whiskey.

Jacks picked up the basics of the game, but Tillie played with practiced ease and won the game in short order. They played another round, setting out tiles and laying walls. Tillie frowned at the board and she drank faster than she had beeb. Jacks wondered what she was seeing there, in the space between walls where they placed small figures.

"This is a good game," Jacks said.

Tillie grunted a response.

"I'm sorry about your daughter," Jacks said. "You must miss her."

"Don't talk about my daughter," Tillie said.

"Sorry, I just wanted—"

Tillie flinched, turned her face away. "Don't."

Jacks shut her mouth. Added tiles and walls to the game board. Tillie's attention drifted away from the game. She reached for the shotgun, cradled it in her lap. Passed out there, loaded. Snored loudly. Jacks put the game pieces back in the box. Wondered how much Tillie needed to throw this in with the bed and the bike. Jacks figured it was worth an extra six bullets. Wanted to give Tillie ammo regardless, a farewell gift on her way to Tucson.

Arthur returned with the bike and the bullet. He left the bike near the threadbare couch and crossed over, eying the passed-out Tillie. He said, "she's really out of it there."

"Yeah." Jacks carried the game back to the table, stashed it in the box. They could offer ten rounds of whole box. Even the best game would get old, with time. Once you'd learned the permeations.

"If she's really out, we could just take this stuff."

"Leave her the bullets," Jacks said.

Arthur grumbled and trudged over to the stair. He put the boxes of ammo on the top step, just behind the bannister. "If we leave 'em here, someone will steal them."

"You wanted to steal her couch."

"She doesn't need her couch. She's heading out of town forever," Arthur said. "She's going to die on her way to Tucson. No doubt about it. She'll die and she'll come back here and the militia will shoot her in the head."

"Pay the woman," Jacks said. "Poor thing's lost enough."

Arthur hovered at the base of the steps, debating whether to keep arguing or cede the ground to Jacks. He made the right decision. "Help me with the couch," he said. "We'll try not to wake her."

The couch was heavier than it looked. The arms sloped in, which made it hard to get a good grip. Jacks got her fingers under the bottom, and the arm sloped out and pushed her against her face.

"Got it?" Arthur said.

"Got it," she said.

Arthur pushed and Jacks retreated, reversing through the cluttered yard.

Tillie roused herself awake with a snort, head fuggy with rye whiskey and grief. She didn't remember falling asleep. She'd been dreaming about Mark and the kids. A nice day, before the world changed. Before the dead were walking. She recognised the weight of the shotgun in her lap. She opened her eyes and blinked at the scene before her: all her furniture in the yard, everything she'd built with Mark. She'd wandered outside in her sleep? It'd happened a lot, since Mark died.

Tillie blinked at tried to focus, remember the last few hours. There were two kids stealing her couch, trying to cart it down the street. Panic brought the adrenaline. Tillie rose to her feet with a shout. "Hey!" she cried. "Thieves! Stop them! They're stealing!"

There were two kids, a boy and a girl. The girl reminded Tillie of her daughter. The right age. The right hair. The right attitude.

The boy dropped and turned, face contorted. He stomped towards the yard, yelling something Tillie couldn't hear. She brought the shotgun up and warned him to back off. Warned him to return her couch.

"We paid you." The kid pointed to the top of the stair. "Your ammo's right there. We paid you."

Tillie squeezed the shotgun trigger and blasted empty air.

Drunk, dammit. Too inebriated to aim. What in hell had she been doing? Why were these damns kids shouting at her? Jesus fucking christ.

Jacks recognised crazy when she saw it, and she knew Tillie had crossed the line. Too much booze, too much grief. Too many crazy plans. Arthur kept shouting, trying to explain. Trying to convince Tillie to put the shotgun down and understand what they were doing.

Tillie didn't waste time. Wasting time got you killed these days. She dropped the couch and took cover behind it. Drew the 9mm as Tillie's attempted to aim, the shotgun waving crazy figure eights through the air in an attempt to draw a bead on Arthur.

"Put the gun down, we paid you," Arthur shouted. "Hell, we'll give you the couch back, lady. What the hell is wrong with you."

Tillie squeezed the trigger a second time. Closer to Arthur this time. Jacks didn't give her a third chance. Drew a bead and lined up her shot. Two rounds to the centre mass, a third to the head, just like they were taught. Stop the momentum and destroy the brain. Easiest way to drop a deader.

Tillie went down hard, blood pooling under her. That was new. The deaders didn't bleed out when you shot them. They just spat flecks of dark gore and dropped to the ground.

Arthur looked back at her. "What did you do?"

Jacks holstered her gun. She surveyed the yard. "Get your bike. Get the games. Get the couch," she said.

Weeks later, the house was abandoned. The stuff Jacks and Arthur didn't take remained in the front yard. Detritus, now. Decaying in the rain.

"This woman was deranged," Arthur said, explaining it to people. "Trying to sell all her stuff, talking about heading to Tucson with the soldiers up in Rocky. We humoured her, and we scored some cool stuff. She played these games with Jacks. It was weird. You found it weird, right, Jacks?"

And Jacks nodded, because he expected it and it *was* weird, just a little. Because *weird* made it easier to accept what she'd done. She wondered what would have happened if Tillie hadn't woken up. Maybe she'd be up in Rocky right now. Maybe she'd be flying to Tucson.

"Yeah," Jack said. "It was all kind of weird."

Then she said, "Anyone in the mood for a game?"

BENEATH THESE TREES, THE DEAD

Marla chews on beef jerky and walks through the orange groves, pretending to look for survivors. She's not serious about the job right now, slouched shoulders and dragged feet. Hands shoved deep into her pockets, glaring at the fruit hanging low on the branches. Autumn harvests grow heavy with the rains, and there's too few willing to pick fruit outside the town walls no matter how well it pays. I'm crouched on the ground, studying the footprints churned through the soft earth. No doubt in my mind what happened here: a lax watch, a hole in the orchard fence, a hungry deader swarm. Marla catches my eye, then looks away. Shines a torch down the next ordered corridor of trees. Swallows her jerky and produces another stick. Marla claims the jerky helps with the smell, but there's no rotting bodies here. Our dead have up and walked away, or they've run and the dead are giving chase.

"This is stupid," Marla says. She tears off a fresh mouthful of jerky, incisors exposed.

"This is the job," I tell her.

"Theres no survivors here." Marla waves at the abandoned baskets, still half-filled with fruit.

"They're paying us to look."

"Sixteen workers."

"We're only looking for one."

"It's not even twenty-four hours, yet. Client had a bad feeling. We shouldn't *be* here yet."

Drool leaks from the corner of Marla's lip and she advances down the orchard, switching the torch back-and-forth. I examine the earth, but I'm no tracker. I can understand the soil when it speaks loud and slow, but as the steps move away from the churn…

My phone chimes. An alert from town, warning us there's dead on the move.

Marla turns back. "Don't," she says.

"We'll need to know if the road back is clear."

"You'll fret. And you fret too much."

I check my phone. The dead are massing on the town's west side, closing on the wall. Local militia gathering to thin the herd, but it'll mean taking the long way back. My brows draw together and my mouth tightens. I turn away so Marla can't see, but she knows me. She knows I'm worried.

"Told you," she says, and spits jerky fluid into the nearby tree root. She swallows, done with the meat, and reaches for an orange to follow. Sharp nails rip into the tough rind, exposes the white pith. Marla divides the edible flesh, devours it. Juice stains her lip, and she tosses the peel without care.

"You're contaminating the scene," I say.

"Like it matters, Eli." She fixes me with her 'scary' look, the one she used when questioning suspects. "We're just a fucking band-aid, yeah?"

"You're the boss. I'm just saying."

Marla throws up her hands and stalks off, following the trees. She leaves a peel trail in her wake, keeps both hands away from the H&K looped over her shoulder, devouring fresh orange and spitting out pips. She heads for the fence line, on the search for the spot where the dead broke in.

I drop a right hand to my pistol and hustle after her, just in case they haven't left yet. We can't go back without confirming the client's fate, even if we know the inevitable result is the same as a hundred other cases.

Marla finds an abandoned bucket three meters from the fence. She says, "Call 'em in."

I close my eyes and draw a slow breath. Draw my Barretta and fire three shots into the air. No silencer to muffle the noise out here, and too few people to create ambient noise. The shots boom through the stillness.

Marla finishes her orange and raise her gun. I put my back against a tree, cover the other direction.

No deaders come to investigate. No shortcuts on this one. I plant my foot and kick the stray bucket away, sending its contents rolling into the dark. Marla doesn't turn around. She raises her hand to signal, demanding stillness, but there's no confrontation here. No demand I knock it off and behave professionally.

Marla doesn't care about this job. It's too close to home.

I hope it doesn't kill us both.

Marla and Walt James and Annalise Johnson, they were cops together. Homicide detectives in the same precinct, back in the days when *how* somebody died ranked higher when they reanimated. They adapted to the new world, built a business around getting answers for folks who still wanted answers when their loved ones disappeared. Marla plays poker with Walt and Melanie every Tuesday night, tries to take three weeks off every year to fish when work and waves of the dead permit recreational excursions. They still consider themselves as good cops. Not bastards, never *bastards*. Not part of the problem, back in ACAB days.

Last September, Marla hired me. I'm not a good cop in any way, but I noticed things, and they taught me stuff. I got pretty good at connecting uneasy feelings with a tangible detail in a scene. For instance, in our last job, Marla took me on a road trip all the way down Nimbin way. Searching for a dead boy who left the town's safety, trusted his fate to permaculture communes established in the belief they can live in peace with the dead. We trekked cross-country with sleeping bags and rifles, surviving on trail mix and jerky. Tracked the dead kid's shambling footsteps to a cannabis farm two clicks out from the compound. Just another job, Marla said. Business as fucking usual.

The dead ambushed us on the way home, just outside the Nimbin walls. Six of 'em broke through the tree line, shambling at furious speed. Too close for rifle work, so we fought them hand-to-hand, scuffling with hatchets and handguns. I copped a black eye from this small fella, a balding corpse determined to rip out my throat and crack my skull with a rock. Marla's opponents scratched her up, long fingernail marks along her forearms. No bites. I ask for visual confirmation, but she assures me everything's okay. "Been doing this since the first rains, kid."

She was the boss, so I went with it. Marla suggested we stay out longer, let our wounds heal before we headed back and answered questions at the wall.

We set up hammocks high in the trees, above the deader's reach if any stumbled over us in the night. Built a fire and traded whisky slugs, just passing the time. Marla tied a belt around her wounded arm, slowing the blood flow. Just in case, she said. Kept an axe ready, just in case we'd misjudged things and had to lop her forearm off before the infection spread.

I slept little that night.

The next few days passed in a restless shamble. We ate sparse meals, drank stale instant coffee, then drained our whisky supplies in the evenings. Moved our camp down the river when our water supplies ran short. It took five days for Marla's wounds to scab. My black eye lost its squint. We drove back to Brisbane a full week overdue, already assumed dead.

Marla reported to the gate guards, submitted to a full inspection. They separated us and asked for a full report, in my own words, without Marlene watching. I told the truth, no big deal. Stupid call, but I didn't go beyond the fence in my old job. All this was Marla's domain.

The gate guards asked me to repeat our exploits. Fretted over Marla's injury, and the fact we'd dawdled on our way home. They brought us together to answer questions again, reconcile our stories. Marla explained our job in a calm, reasonable voice. Ran them through the fight, all the precautions we'd taken. Assured them Walt and Annalise could lock her down at their office, if required. Explained I was just a punk kid, unused to being out in the wide world.

The gate guards nodded and smiled and conferred. They separated us a second time. A short, uniformed guard sat down beside me with a paper ledger and a wan smile. She asked me—honestly—if I was satisfied Marla emerged from the fight unscathed. I assured them of my satisfaction, then assured them I mostly thought it was okay, then admitted I didn't give it much thought either way. She was in charge. I trusted my boss.

The gate guards put us in quarantine. Three weeks, mandatory.

I figured quarantine was a standard operating procedure, not a big deal at all. They stashed us in an apartment block in the no-man's-land between the two fence lines. Warned us not to roam unless we wanted to get shot. The rooms were sparse: beds, a chair, seventeen old paperbacks on a rickety shelf. Nothing to do but read or sleep, and I elected to get some shuteye. I wasn't awake for Marla's departure, but I roused myself as she slipped inside again. Caught her rummaging through the bare kitchen, searching for a glass, an unopened scotch in her fist.

"Thirsty?" She tilted a fresh bottle my way.

I jabbered my surprise, astonished she'd risked a trip on our first night.

"Went for supplies." Marla jabbed the scotch bottle towards the fence. "Walt dropped food and booze over. Something better than dried meat and trail mix for breakfast."

She warned soup over a small camp stove. Creamy tomato from a tin. Marla devoured hers with great appetite, finished mine when I struggled to eat.

She belched and took the dishes away. Grabbed a book and retreated to her room. I stood in the small kitchenette, worried about the job for the first time. Worried about her lax approach to safety and the implications given our job.

I reload my beretta and join Marla at the orchard fence, going left when she goes right. She's dressed for the heat, this trip. Bare shoulders, sweat beading and rolling down her arm. Scar tissue across her forearm, pale in the full moonlight. She's got her rifle at the ready now, held tight against her shoulder. I hold my gun and flashlight together, advance thirty meters looking for tracks.

"We could go back to the car," I say, voice low.

Marla raises her gun and turns. "Lot of off-road driving to get around patrols. Not much space to manoeuvre if the dead corner us."

"Take 'em time to break through the glass, though. Give us a chance to thin their numbers some."

Carla touched her forearm, shifts her stare to the path back. "You got anything on your side?"

"Nada."

"I do." She jerks her rifle towards the fence. "Fence's pulled down here. Think they left the same way they came in, with some extra bodies in the mix."

"Damn." I scrubbed my forehead, loathing the heat. "You figure she's dead?"

"Dead or not, we're following the tracks." Marla hoisted her pack and gestured. "Gotta check whether the clients among them."

Pistol takes lead in low-vis terrain. Small guns are built for up-close work, rifles take down at range. Means my job is keeping the deaders off Marla while she thins the herd with precision shooting.

Marla's no crackshot when she's got it all together, but I'm not much better. Junior partner gets the pistol. Marla gets the Remington.

I keep the fence on my left side, eyes scanning the darkness. Marla tramps behind me. She's eating again, forever hungry. Neither of us speaks. Neither of us wants to be out here solo, not when tracks are this fresh. Too many chances to get bit, to get your escapes routes cut off without warning. We're halfway around the orchard when I stop and break out the canteen. The tracks are muddier here. Inevitable result when multiple drag their weight along, no longer lifting their feet. The dead are heading away from the orchard, into the overgrown scrub.

I cap my water and exhale a sigh. Marla gnaws a jerky lump free and masticates the dried flesh with purpose.

"We don't have to be here," I tell her.

"Say what?"

She speaks with her mouthful. Smacks her lips as chewing resumes. My skin crawls, and I adjust my grip.

"We know what happened," I tell her. "We can just go. Get paid, yeah?"

"We don't know. We can make a good guess," Marla says. "They're paying us to be *sure*."

I study the night-dark scrub, the hill's slow incline. When I don't push off voluntarily, Marla lurches into motion. Sweat stains her singlet, and I wonder if she might come down with something. It takes effort to swallow my fear and follow. Illness freaks us all out now we know where it can lead.

"Come on," Marla says. "Rattle ya dags."

She's in charge, and she surges into the darkness. Ignoring protocol, waving her torchlight around, keeping her rifle close. I follow her, dragging my feet.

When Marla glances over her shoulder to check I've got her back, she knows my heart's not in it.

Marla believes in the mission. Believes in giving people answers and closure. A chance to grieve instead of hope. She thinks we all need an ending these days, no ragged edges left to tatter as time eats away at our resolve. She believes in it with a fury, so I kinda believe in it too, following her sweaty shoulders downhill despite my strong misgivings. We find the dead twenty minutes into the hike. Sixteen corpses shambling through the night, heading towards the town. Marla signals and we split up, taking positions down the slope and picking the field of engagement. The dead are many things, but they aren't smart and we've got the drop on them. Five minutes and our gunfire thins their numbers. Marla takes down far more than I do.

No injuries. Always a cause for celebration on a trip. Marla picks her way through the vanquished corpses, produces a battered phone and photographs the client. We drag her corpse away from the others, dig a grave and bury her. Marla photographs that too, then we hike back to the car.

We're still cut off from town, which means they'll take precautions when we get home. Another quick trip through quarantine. 48 hours, this time. I don't bat an eyelid when Marla breaks out the first night—it's all too familiar now.

We do our time. We got back home. Marla delivers the bad news and collects our money, delivers my half without a word.

There's a week off after the orchard job. Downtime where Marla and I recharge, get a break from one another. I buy drinks at the town pub. Eat breakfast at the Montague Road diner. I kill time. We all kill time, these days, whiling away the empty hours until the end of the world catches up with us.

Marla drops me a letter on the sixth day, warning me there's a new gig on its way. A client eager to know what happened to the missing son. A soldier stationed up the coast, a two-week trip all the way to Rockhampton. Trips via car take extra planning and set-up costs, but they pay off if we can deliver.

I call by her house to get the details. "How long?" I ask.

"Another week. They've got our quote, they're just debating how much it's really worth to them."

"But they'll say yes?"

"They always say yes, Rook. Best you pack, yeah?"

I don't want to go north with Marla, but I don't know how to say no.

My buddy Arlo joined the militia the first year of high school. Stayed with it long after our cohort fulfilled our mandatory hours and passed basic weapons training. We still meet up every Thursday, if we're both free. Catching up for beers and dinner at the pub where Arlo's drunk free since he turned seventeen.

Everybody loves the militia these days, thanks 'em for their sacrifice. All the girls love Arlo now. What the hell's up with that?

Arlo's two drinks in the bag when I find him, but he consents to let me buy the next round. Lays claim to a small, cast-iron table out in the pub's beer garden.

I bring him a glass of the pub's cheap homebrew and tell him what's on my mind.

"Boss wants me to go up the coast," I tell him. "Rocky. Grain Country. Military client."

"Jeez," Arlo says. "I'm sorry, mate."

There's a tone the militia boys get when they're pretending they don't know nothing. "Spill," I tell him.

"Nothing to spill," he says.

"We had a close call, me and Marla," I tell him. "First out of town job we did together. Got thrown in quarantine for weeks."

Arlo scanned the crowd, attention already shifting to potential companionship for the night. "Quarantine officers will do that. For the good of the herd," he says.

"Taught me something important: my boss is fucking crazy."

We finish our drinks, and I buy another round. Two girls walk past our table, and Arlo puts on a brave face for 'em. Chest puffed out, the fearless militiaman blessed with a cheeky smile.

I dredge up the question I don't want to ask: "How do we know if quarantine fails?"

Arlo's gaze dragged away from the two girls, face screwed up in mild confusion. He asks me to repeat the question.

"We know because there's deaders," he says.

"Nah, not like that." I grope for an explanation. "If someone's bit, but they hide the injury. If they sneak something in the quarantine teams don't catch. What happens if someone's bit, but it's still incubating inside 'em?"

Arlo's smile fades. "The Clementine sisters." His brow furrows with the effort of dredging up the memory. "Twins outta Melbourne, just after the fall. First major outbreak in a secure camp, thirty-seven days after the most recent rain. They switched places during the physical, disguised the bite on the older sister's arm. Outbreak six years later, when the elder sister died during a bar brawl. Sixty-seven dead before the local squads controlled the outbreak."

His frown lingers a moment longer, but a barmaid ambles over with two fresh beers on her tray. "From the redhead at the bar. She'd like a chat when you're free, yeah?"

Arlo beams at the news. He flashes me a questioning look, wondering if I'm done.

"So, we can't detect it?" I say. "Once the virus is in the bloodstream, there's no knowing if someone's infected until they're dead? The virus just sits there, waiting?"

"That's the theory," Arlo says. "Now, if you'll excuse me…"

He abandons the table and the half-drunk beer, sliding over to the smiling admirers, ramping up the charm.

I don't think I've finished a conversation with Arlo since he put on the uniform.

I walk home from the pub, my route idling along the safe zone and the fence line. The boundary where the town's defences give way to wheat and rice fields, to vegetable patches and the large paddocks filled with dairy cattle. Fields observed by guard towers and militia patrols, the town's lifeblood, every inch well-lit and protected twenty-four hours of every day.

Beyond the fields, the town's abandoned suburbs. Beyond them, the scrub and the orchards. The slow stretch towards the allied farms and settlements we can reach on foot, then the rare farm still running a vehicle. We learned our lessons soon after the first rain, know the dangers inherent in living clumped together, everyone stacked on top of each other. I hear rumours there're still folks holed up in the cites, where the dead have the numbers advantage, but the smart money's in a small town. A place where you can know your neighbours, gauge how far you trust them to obey security protocols.

It's a warm night. Humid. Clouds are gathering off the coast. There's fresh rain coming, fresh infections to bring the deaders up from the earth. A good night to get inside and stay there, to check on neighbours and make sure they're safe.

A stranger fall in behind me and follows me all seven blocks between the pub and home. I try crossing to the far side of the street and they follow. I vary my pace, and they do the same. My fingers itch for the beretta at my hip, but I tell myself its paranoia.

He's a big guy. Blue jeans and a long-sleeve shirt, sneakers with holes at the toe. He comes up beside me, flashes a toothy grin. "Nice night for it."

"If you say so."

"I do." He grins at me again, expecting a response. He's flossy, eyes glazed. I'm not sure how many drinks he's had, but he's edging up on the line where drunk becomes aggressive.

"Rain's coming," I tell him. "Can't stay nice for much longer."

He casts an eye towards the horizon and mops a forearm against his brow. He steps closer and nudges my arm.

"My cousin got caught in the rains last month. She's still breathing. Hasn't said nothing to no-one yet. Begged me to keep my trap shut."

I'm not sure how to respond. I venture a muted, "Okay."

"Can't let the bastards run your life," he says.

"Well, no. You can. You should," I tell him.

"What the fuck you say?"

"We're all in this together," I tell him.

The stranger grabs my arm, dragging me to a halt. He's taller than me. Heavier. Well fed. "She got caught in the *rain*." His voice vibrates with anger. "What the fuck's wrong with you, man?"

His fingers curl into a fist. I can tell he's ready to lash out, looking for an excuse.

My hand's already on the gun. I pull it free and wave it in his face, force him to back off.

"Nobody's making these rules to fuck with you," I tell him. "They're keeping us all safe, you idiot."

They buried our orchard client on a Thursday afternoon. Closed casket, so nobody knows how she died. Rocks in the coffin to give it weight. The family pretends it's an accident, not an encounter with the dead. I find a seat up the back and wait, watching the guests filter in. Guests arrive in dribs and drabs. Chairs scrape against the polished floor. Family members find each other, weeping. Others huddle on the fringes, sullen and angry. Death isn't special anymore. Everyone's gunned down a loved one or a friend, knows they might have to kill more if the rains don't stop. But we're here. We respect the process, and we nod at the memorials. We all agree it's a damn shame.

It's hot out, when the mourning's done. Muggy, steam rising off the pavement. The mourners gather on the front steps to trade memories of the deceased. A haggard woman in a white cotton dress holds forth on the danger the rains present. "Man keeled over on Vine last night. Heart attack, just before the rain hit. Take comfort in that, Edie. Nowhere is safe anymore. This fella on Vine keeled over and died in the storm, and it took half the militia to put the dead down after he started feeding. Katie, at least, she rests in peace. She's not one of *them*…"

I retreat a few steps down the churchyard. Heat radiates from the concrete, but folks wander off all the same. Nobody drives in town anymore. We walk, or we bike everywhere. There's a headache forming, a painful spike just behind my left eye.

I nudge the woman in white cotton. "We're all going to be a deader, sooner or later. No way to avoid it."

The client's mother recognises me. Frowns at my intervention.

The woman in white cotton holds forth, regardless. "I've known Katie since before the rains," she says. "She wanted to help people. We all knew the orchard job was dangerous, but she swore it mattered, anyway. 'No point surviving the dead if we all die of scurvy, auntie,' she'd tell me. Damn shame it got her this way."

Marla's on my doorstep twenty-four hours later. "Job's on. We're going to Rocky. Grab your kit and let's get driving."

She's chewing jerky again. For a moment, I flash on a sinister alternative. A lump of flesh torn off a neighbour. A little something to ward off the hunger. It's stupid, but it gets me wondering. What if the dead are smarter than us? What if, one day, they're smart enough to crack our safe little shells?

"This is my last gig," I tell Marla. "I can't keep doing this."

"Bullshit. You've got a talent for it."

"No," I tell her. "I've had enough."

She meets my gaze, still chewing. One hand resting against her gun. "Rational mind wants to believe that's true, but you love it," she says. "You'll live for this shit, Rookie. You're just dealing with the first year nerves."

I head inside and gather my gear for a long-term trek in the wild. Rations. Weapons. Clothes. Marla's sourced us a four-wheel drive for the run, its roof racks loaded up with gear. I stop by the kitchen and finish my coffee. Luke-warm. Hickory flavoured. A little pleasure bought with the money I earned after the orchard job.

Marla hits the kitchen and drapes an arm across my shoulder. "Rattle your dags," she says. "It's time."

Her breath is hot against my ear. Her voice low, a predators rasp. She keeps rattling off orders, prodding me into motion. I've already put my coffee down, gathered my stuff. Marla calls for me to move faster. I block her out as we load up the car. She's eager to be out there, beyond the wall's confines and other people's scrutiny. She really, truly loves this shit.

I tie my last bag to the roof and sigh. "Come on. Let's get this over with."

LAST DRINKS

My buddy Del Winnick held the floor, waving a martini glass half-full of cheap piss. Del Winnick's a dab hand with a .303, so nobody ever tells him to shut his mouth, even when they should.

We're on the thirteenth floor of the Aloha Sunrise, emptying the last bottles from the hotel bar. Dark clouds gathered on the horizon, bringing in a fresh round of rain. The dead were already thick on the ground. We'd locked the Aloha down to buy ourselves some time, but we weren't getting out. That window had closed.

There was Del and me and my second wife, Gracie. Del's current fella, Richie, who'd come into our lives after Del's wife got eaten when the dead first rose. Del and Gracie and me were locals, which meant we'd lived on the Gold Coast for years, even if we started elsewhere. The new guy, Richie, claimed to be local in the other way. Born here, raised here, never left. Rare as hen's teeth on the Gold Coast, especially now so many are dead.

The booze was Richie's plan. Red wine, because the whites were warm these days. Cocktail glasses to lend things a touch of class, and because the proper glasses were long gone. We'd drained two bottles of Wolf Blass cab sav, and started on the shiraz we'd been saving. None of us had been properly drunk for a while, not the way we drank that day.

We'd spent a year pretending Del and Richie weren't screwing, and we weren't doing that no more. Gracie asked, and Del held forth, telling us about his great loves and conquests from the time before the rains. Women, yes, but men too. Del fell in love with a veterinary student at uni, and they'd spent six months screwing after their Animal Production and Welfare lectures instead of revising their notes and doing the readings. "Gods, that kid was beautiful," Del said. Red wine spilled out of his glass. "We were both so damn young and beautiful then. Not like I am today."

"You're pretty enough," Richie said, quietly.

Richie said little, generally.

Gracie spotted an opportunity and launched into a story. Told us about the man she'd married before she and I met. They'd lived together for six years, back in the late seventies. Gracie said, "Talbot used to play in bands. He was lead guitar in this group. Everyone figured they were the next big things. Radio play off their first single. Tour of the US playing with the Stones. Made good money doing that, but he got hooked and everything went down the shitter."

Del and I nodded. We both knew Talbot was a junkie, and Gracie liked to talk about it.

"I miss radio," Del said. "And the Stones."

Richie cut in. "Sunday afternoons with a joint and Exile on Main Street playing on vinyl."

Their eyes met, and a moment of heat passed between them. Gracie looked to me, hot with anger. Interruptions were a pet peeve, and she'd never liked Del. Had less reason to hide it now, but instincts die hard even at the end of everything.

"This is why The Children left." Gracie jabbed an accusing finger at Richie and Del. "This, right here, drove them away."

Del Winnick's dark-haired and hawk-nosed, at ease with himself, sixty-eight years old. Fit before the dead arrived, slimmer now we've survived a few months. Daily cardio and limited carbs do wonders, even for lard-asses like me. They're fucking magic for assholes like Del, already used to burning calories.

When sober, Del's a good guy. Articulate and personable. Went into law after vet studies fell through, made use of his golden tongue.

Drunk, he was combative. "The Children left because they were punks. And because they thought we'd get them killed. We're too old and slow to survive, you know?"

He said it with an exaggerated wink, sloshing a fresh slug of red into our glasses. Gracie bit her tongue. She'd had children with her first husband, but they were long dead before the rains. She had little patience for assholes, and Del showed his ass more and more these days.

"Maddison told me we should eat rat poison," I said. "There's a supply down on the eighth floor. She'd been stockpiling it for her kids."

"Fuck the rat poison," Gracie said. "And fuck Maddison's kids."

We were all testy about The Children. Our collective name for our fellow survivors, men and women in their twenties and thirties and forties. Other residents of the Aloha who recently migrated inland rather than hold this place.

Richie slouched back in his chair. He extended both feet under the table. "Which one was Maddison?"

"The blonde," I said. "Short hair, missing an eye."

"Ah," Richie said. "Her."

Del leaned over the table, resting his elbows against the plastic. He glanced from me to Gracie to Richie, eyes bright with anticipation. "Fucking pain in the ass, that one. Probably talked the kids into abandoning the city, fucking off to God knows where."

Gracie spared a glance for the gathered dead below us, pushing against the barricade sealing the Aloha from nearby streets. "Not like she was wrong," she said.

"This? This is nothing." Flecks of spit darted across the table as Del stoked his anger. "If we had a full crew, we could hold this off. Pick off the deaders as they close in, thin out the herd and take them hand-to-hand. That bitch—"

"She wasn't a bitch," I said.

"That bitch." Del fixed me with an angry glare. "She said we're to blame for all this. Everyone our age. Said if the zombies didn't get us, climate change or pandemics would. No fucking personal responsibility, always blaming someone else for fucking her life up. Bet she coaxed the others into walking. Brainwashed them into leaving us here."

Gracie bumped my knee with hers. She turned an expectant look my way. Gracie hated Maddison, thought I was too close to the younger woman, but Gracie had no patience for Del's angry self-pity. The enemy of her enemy was worth defending.

Usually I tried to extend Del the benefit of the doubt. He'd lost folks, more than Gracie and me. And maybe he loved Richie, here at the end, but he'd been with his wife Anna for decades. He'd been angrier since she got eaten. A changed man, and less reasonable.

Hell, we were all different now. Not so together and self-assured as we'd been in the before-times. My former self would have shrugged off Gracie's urging, unwilling to rock the boat. Now, I hit my limit. Wasn't like there were many more chances.

I fixed Del with a hard look. "Maddison wasn't a bitch," I said. "She took care of me and Gracie, back when all this started. Brought us food when I twisted my ankle and couldn't scavenge for a stretch. She thought ahead and saw a problem, and she proposed a solution. Everyone voted on it, and implemented it as a group."

"I didn't vote for it," Del said. "None of us did."

Gracie reached for the shiraz. "I did."

"Bullshit," Del said. "You hated her."

"I did, but they were right to go." Gracie poured another drink. "They were right to leave your ass, too. We've picked the supermarkets clean, and going house-to-house for tinned food wouldn't feed a group our size. There's no reason to stay."

"It's home," Del growled. "We raised our kids here."

"My kids are dead," Gracie said. "Where I raised them doesn't matter now."

Del snarled and pitched his martini glass at the wall, staining the beige paint with red wine. "Then why in fuck are you here?" he said. "Why didn't you go with them?"

"Because you're my friend," I told him. "And I knew you wouldn't leave. You're a dick, but we've had a good innings, mate, and I'm tired. If we make a last stand, I'm happy with how it ends. We had a good life, all four of us, if you exclude the last few years."

"If." Del snorted. He went inside to find another glass, returned with an empty peanut butter jar and a bottle of shitty pinot we'd liberated from one of the Petersons abandoned units two doors down the hall.

"If this was before," Del said, "I'd kick your ass out for being a dick."

"If this was before, I'd go."

We stared at one another, refusing to back down. Del wasn't used to me standing up to him, calling him out on his shit. Before. The word triggered memories. Nostalgia. Before was a time prior to the dead rising, hungry for the flesh of the living. Before, everything made sense. Before, we didn't think about the future.

Before, we owned the world and bent it to our desires.

Down below, on the streets, the dead gathered. Hundreds of them pressed against the barricade, moaning, eager to get inside. We drank and pretended they weren't there, or that we might yet find some way out. There wasn't one. We'd left it too long to make the call. Now the dead surrounded us. We were stuck with each other and the rat poison.

Gracie reached for the pinot. "Time for a refill," she said.

The clouds were dark and heavy as they inched towards the city. The towers of the Gold Coast stood resolute. We'd fenced off the Aloha, but there were hundreds of high-rise resorts all along the strip. Palm trees swayed in the afternoon breeze, and the waves rolled in like they always did. The walking dead, fourteen floors below, swarmed the fence like tiny ant-sized people. They didn't need to be dead at all, when seen from this height. Ignore the moans and the fingers clawing at the metal barricade, and it could have been just another lazy Saturday. Retirement in a patch of paradise, a reward for our decades of work.

Richie took point this time. He raised his glass and grinned at Del. I got the vibe they wished we weren't there with 'em, but safety in numbers, even dwindling numbers, took precedence over libido. "To the fucking end of the world," Richie said. "And not sharing it with ungrateful pricks who made off with all the good shit."

He swilled back a mouthful of pinot. The rest of us followed suit. I'd never been a red wine drinker, but histamine problems weren't top of mind anymore. Tomorrow would take care of itself.

"I'll tell you the thing that irritates me," Del said. "It didn't have to be this way. We're not unreasonable. If they gave us time, we would have listened. If they laid out the plan, I might have volunteered to stay behind and give them a fighting chance. Anthony's right, we've had a good innings. I've lost enough. But they left us here, surplus to requirements."

He drained his wine and topped up his jar, emptying the bottle. The rest of us nursed our drinks. The Children gave us a choice. Me and Gracie, at least. They even asked Del to vote, although they knew it would pass by the time he weighed in. They'd argued the pros and cons without him. Del might think he's reasonable, but the rest of us knew better. He wasn't pissed about losing; he was pissed at being left out of the debate. Maddison and his friends knew letting him weigh in turned the whole thing into a circus. Del would string things out, win on a technicality. And they knew he wouldn't leave. They'd checked with me, just to be sure, and I'd confirmed he'd stay.

We pretended we couldn't hear the dead. My knee brushed against Gracie's knee, and I was just drunk enough to wish we had time for more touching before the end arrived.

"I'm not a fucking relic," Del said. "I kept fit, before all this started. I can outrun half the punks who left. Lawrence? Two years of this and that kid is still huffing and puffing his way through a two-K run. Lawrence was fucking twenty-three when the rains began. He created videos for tickytok."

"TikTok," Gracie corrected.

"The fuck it matters!" Del slammed his jar against the table. Pinot splashed over the lip. He sucked his fingers clean and thought about his words. "Lawrence made videos for a living."

"Content," I said.

Del turned on me, brow furrowed. This was his version of making peace, and I'd nudged a toe against a landmine. I raised both hands up, surrendering. "Video's a medium. Film too," I said. "You think Lawrence knows how to work with anything not stored on his phone?"

"*Lawrence made fucking videos,*" Del repeated. He wanted us to shut up and listen to his ramble, reassert his authority over the conversation. Gracie and I exchanged a look, buttoned our mouths and let him talk. Del waved a hand at the view. "Tell me what the fuck making videos is going to do in a world like this?"

"You were a lawyer," Gracie said. "Drafted any contracts lately?"

Del adopted a pious expression. "Lawyers negotiate. We're always useful."

Richie surprised us all, butting in with a grin: "If you'd been a nurse, they would have kidnapped your ass instead of leaving us behind, though."

Del blinked, taken aback. Richie didn't speak much, never contradicted Del. They'd been together for thirteen months now, moved in together after the first two weeks. Build a home in the Aloha, filling the gaps left behind when Del's family died. It brought Del something akin to happiness. He enjoyed being the loud one, the talker and decider.

It was hard not to read something into Richie speaking up. Maybe we were really fucked. Nothing left to lose.

Richie leaned across and kissed Del on the lips. "I love you, mate, but we're not that fucking useful. They left us because we'd slow them down."

The betrayal hit Del hard. He believed The Children left us for the wrong reasons. Because we were old, too slow, too stubborn. Del considered that choice an oversight—wasn't he still the best shot remaining? He'd hunted throughout his years as a lawyer, and Richie worked construction. Built half the barricade on the ground floor, shored up the weaknesses.

Me, I'd taught sixth grade, and Gracie managed a support center. Del believed we all possessed valuable skills, and The Children would come to regret their mistake. He believed we'd built fences with these people. The Children. We'd built fences and built a community, generators to keep the electricity on and the elevators running. Sniper squads to thin the herds when a fresh wave charged the barricade, and a militia to hold the deaders off when things got up close and personal.

We had the freedom to walk the Aloha precinct without fear because men like him took command and men like Richie built a wall.

Del didn't want to hear about sustainability, or what needed to happen to keep us alive long-term. We were in our sixties, fighting zombies. We had, what, a decade left? Every time The Children suggested we move, Del argued there were alternatives. "We'll find another solution," he said. "We're smart. We've got the resources."

My mistake was trying to be reasonable. "Look," I said. "We're not who we used to be."

"I'm worth ten of fucking Lawrence," Del said.

"Doesn't change the fact you're sixty-eight, and Lawrence is twenty-three." Richie patted Del's arm, then leant over for a kiss. "We both get up to pee in the night, and we haven't had sunscreen in a year. What happens when one of us gets melanoma and there's no-one to cut it out? Or when one of us breaks a leg, and the bones are slow to heal?"

Del slumped in his seat and glowered. He didn't want to hear it. But, truth is, we'd all changed since the dead rose. Gracie used to be a plump woman, and I carried twenty kilos I shouldn't, but we were all bone-thin and hungry now. Her apple cheeks were sunken, and her long hair tangled from lack of showering. She still wore gold hoops, one in each ear. Impractical if the dead got close, but Gracie didn't care. "If they're close enough to rip my earrings, they deserve to eat me," she always said.

I respected her attitude, but I'll admit those hoops worried me every time we held off the walking dead.

Red lightning flashed over the ocean. I counted six seconds before the thunder arrived, rumbling like the voice of God, warning of trouble coming. I glanced over the balcony rail. Figured there were three hundred deaders down on the ground, four times what the Aloha could handle back when everyone lived here. Now there were the four of us, plus the other stragglers who'd elected not to leave. Older folks gathered in other parts of the building, holed up in their private farewells. Old neighbors who'd retired here, just like Del and Gracie and me. We'd all lived in the Aloha for years, long enough to recognize faces, but it wasn't until the dead rose that any of us bothered to learn names.

The Gold Coast was that kind of place, before. Nobody moved here for the community and sense of neighborhood. You lived here for the surf and the sun and the golf courses and world-class shopping. That choice made sense before the dead started walking. Now I wished we could have gone with the kids, found a little happiness in the mountains, building a community out of nothing.

"Maybe Maddison was right," I said. "Rat poison might be a better choice than dealing with the dead. We could go out on our terms instead of being ripped to pieces."

"Bullshit," Del said. "That's not who we are."

Gracie rolled her eyes. "Who are we, then?"

"We," Del said, "are battlers. We fought for a better world and we got it, for a while. Nobody's taking that away from me. And I don't feel fucking old, do you?"

Nobody disagreed with him. I didn't feel old. Not even now. My back hurt and my knees hurt and I groped for words I couldn't remember sometimes. I didn't run as fast as I once did, but it ain't like the dead are sprinters. I still felt like a young guy, just one who felt a lot of pain and didn't move so good anymore.

Maybe I had a little fight in me. "I don't hate the idea of going out in a blaze of glory," I said.

"They left us here to die," Del said. "We're going to die fucking well."

"I don't even know how they did it," Richie said. "How in hell didn't we hear it being planned?"

"Text chains," I said. "TikTok."

"I thought the internet went away."

"The Americans brought it back," I said. "And we didn't have time to figure it out."

"The Americans." Del snorted his contempt. The rest of us agreed. "The Americans started all this," Del said. "Dollars to donuts, it started in one of their labs. They wanted the rains and the walking dead."

Agreeing with Del is easier than trying to argue he's full of shit. Downstairs, the dead breeched the outer barricade, shambling in through the gap where sheer weight of numbers pulled down the chain-link fence. There's so many of them out there, fighting to get in.

Who knew they'd become such a problem of late? Their numbers building while nobody paid attention, then swelled when a succession of red rains hit the coast.

And that was the thing, wasn't it? Arguing with Del took time, and we had too little of it to waste.

"We fight, then," Del said. "We hold this place. We make it through the storm and we come out the other side and we rebuild, yeah? We show them we were right to stay. We live better than they ever could."

Gracie and I exchanged a glance. Richie raised an eyebrow.

"Let's have another drink," I said. "Make an evening of it."

It's worth noting we held things together after the rains began. We locked down and stayed inside our homes, listened to the warnings about contagion and close proximity to those infected. Watched the death tolls rise, the breakdowns as hospitals were overwhelmed, transformed into charnel houses where the walking dead found a steady supply of snacks and raw recruits. We railed against the government for doing too little and suspected our neighbors of hoarding too much.

We started out well, then slowly, eventually, the world broke down and we built something new in its place. The dead were numerous, yes, but they were slow and they could be diverted or held back. We could put up fences and barricades to hold them off, train ourselves to use weapons that split the skull. We formed militias and enclaves that worked together, trading with the other survivors who'd organized and rebuilt.

Richie opened the second pinot and topped up everyone's glass. I got that languid, flossy sensation that sits between inebriation and a full-fledged drunk. I grinned at Gracie and touched her hand. She pulled her fingers away and stared at the gathering clouds.

"We should toast," she said. "To our survival."

"Short though it may be," Del said.

"To survival," we said, and touched glasses. Del sloshed a little pinot over the lip of his jar, leaving a trail of red droplets across the plastic balcony table. We all stared at one another, in no hurry to finish our drinks. When the wine was over, it was time to go down and fight. These were the last good times. There were no more when they were done.

"I fought this case a few years back," Del said. "I mean, it wasn't a big thing. I didn't do trial law. I argued contracts and looked over legislation. But I fought this one, because it mattered. Because it was the right thing."

He poured the last of the pinot, confident we'd humor him. Richie offered a benign smile. I wondered if he was placating Del, or genuinely cared for him. Gracie fidgeted in her chair, glancing over the balcony rail. The dead were getting louder now. They were going to break the second barricade soon, and the drinking part of the day would be over.

"We were supposed to be taking in refugees," Del said. "We weren't, because this is Australia. Because we made it easy on ourselves and stashed new arrivals off-shore, kept them cycling through bullshit bureaucracy and living in a hellhole. They called it a deterrent to keep people from trying to come here, and our firm decided this is how we'd all do our thirty-five hours pro bono for the year. I argued this case for a girl named Darya. Mother of two. A make-up artist. She'd been hired for a film in her homeland, found out they were shooting porn too late. Punishable by death, back home. They came after her and her husband. Arrested him, and damn near beat him to death. She came all the way to Australia with two kids, just trying to stay alive, and they dumped her in a compound on a shitty island somewhere north of Cairns. Three fucking years in detention, while people told her she wasn't in danger if she went back home."

Gracie and I exchanged a look. "Well, someone's fucking drunk," Gracie said.

"I'm just talking," Del said. "I've been thinking about her. All the things I could think about, and she's the thing I keep coming back to. Just how fucking unfair it was."

"Did you get her out?" Richie, asking the question. Del stared at him, eyes glimmering, on the verge of tears.

Gracie stood and touched Richie's shoulders. "We might need another bottle," she said. "Wanna see what we can scrounge?"

Richie's glance flicked from Gracie to Del. He switched back and offered a grateful smile. "Tsu brothers in 1402 had a stash. More than they could have taken with them, I think. And they left their keys."

Gracie and Richie disappeared. Del sucked in a long, unsteady breath and his shoulders quivered like he might cry. "I have nightmares about her, trapped," he said. "Stuck there, when all this started. Thinking it couldn't get much worse."

"They probably let them out," I said. "Shit like this, they open the gates, yeah?"

Del reached out, and I took his hand. We sat there, watching the storm roll in. The rain growing closer, bloody and dark.

"If I'm wrong, it would have been fast," I said. "No waiting. It's not much, but it's something."

"You always were a miserable cunt," Del said. "No wonder the kids left us behind."

"That's how it goes," I said.

Del wept. Quiet, heaving sobs as he let the anger out. He was afraid, and he wasn't sure what to do with fear. Never found a useful way to deal with anything he couldn't out-argue or shout down if things got bad. I sat there, holding his hand, letting him get it out of his system.

Richie and Gracie were in the hall. We both caught Gracie's laughter. Del slipped his hand free. He took a deep breath and exhaled, pretended everything was fine. "We really should have gone with them," he said. "That girl, Maddison, was right."

"That girl was forty-six," I told him. "She had time to learn a few things."

"I don't know why I'm like this," Del said. "I don't know who I am anymore."

Gracie elbowed her way through the door, carrying two bottles of Big & Bold shiraz. Cheap plonk, but it would do.

"We hit pay dirt," Gracie said.

"Great!" Del said.

Richie swept in and kissed Del on the lips. He whispered an apology. Gracie sat beside me, placed her bounty on the table.

"Del doesn't know who he is anymore," I said.

"Jesus, join the club. I used to be so many people," Gracie said. "Work Gracie. Home Gracie. Gym Gracie. Another fucking team meeting Gracie."

"Gracie who wore that short skirt to parent teacher night when her kids were busted," I said. "Distracting the teachers to keep 'em out of trouble."

"I had good legs," Gracie said.

"I'll drink to that," I said.

"We've done plenty of drinking," she said. "Any more, and we'll all forget how to use a gun."

Richie twisted the top off the shiraz. "Last drinks, folks. Finish up and we'll go make a fight of this."

We were all drunk; I know that. I couldn't focus real clear. The storm clouds were over the city now, pregnant with impending rain. There'd be more dead on the ground real soon. No way the barricades on the Aloha would hold. We'd go down or the dead would come up, and maybe getting it over with was the right call.

None of us got up to collect our guns, but Del drained his drink in one gulp.

"God," he said. "This is fucking awful."

"We might make it through," Gracie said cheerfully. "Wait out the storm, head into the hills tomorrow. Find somewhere more secure."

"Start over somewhere we can grow," I said. Madeline's words. Gracie and I exchanged a meaningful look.

Del gripped the arm of his chair real tight. He looked at Richie, then looked away. "Anna should be here," he said. Anna was his dead wife. He hadn't spoken about her in months.

The storm clouds loomed over us, dark and crimson. Warm as Satan's butt crack, stirring up the dead, eager for what the rains meant. New deaders rose with every storm, lurching to life and going on the hunt. More people went crazy, carrying out desperate plans to survive the next twenty-four hours.

We drank the last two bottles of shiraz. Richie laid the empties on the side, fallen soldiers taking their last rest. The rain hammered the city, made it hard to talk without raising our voice.

Down below, the second row of barricades protested as the weight of the dead threatened to pull them down. Del stood and peered over the balcony rail.

"Guess it's time," he said.

"I'll load the guns," Richie said. "Let's do it."

But Richie didn't get up. None of us were reaching for weapons or getting up to do jack shit.

Del considered his empty peanut butter jar and the empty bottles. He tossed them over the balcony, let them fall fourteen floors to the gathering dead below. The first spits of rain broke over the city, cold and bloody red. "Last chance to come up with a brilliant plan capable of saving us all."

We all sat there looking at one another, our breathing ragged and our pulses thumping. I could hear the moans of the dead below, the groan of the building as they pressed against it, trying to pull it down. I could hear the dead as we all sat there, not budging an inch, not even when the rain grew harder and drenched everything on the balcony.

The dead would soon be inside, surging up the stairs. We were goners. Me and Del and Gracie. Del's lover Richie, who was not his wife. We were all on the clock now, soon to be eaten.

Del waited for the brilliant plan that meant we didn't have to change or fight.

AUTHORS NOTE

ORIGIN STORY

If there are four things I truly love in this world, they are my spouse, my cats, writing weird books, and designing book covers.

This book was born because of the last thing on that list. See, back in 2022 I lost my job. I wasn't particularly phased—I've spent most of my life freelancing, so I knew I could build up my income through a combination of different gigs.

What I needed was some short-term cash to tide me over until regular gigs flowed in, so I started designing pre-made covers and selling them to other publishers.

Usually, when I design a book cover for GenrePunk Books or Brian Jar Press, I know a few things about the book in advance. Not just the genre, but the mood and feel of the story. The kind of people who are likely to enjoy it, and what else they're likely to be reading.

These are incredibly useful from a design perspective, because they give you a framework you can work to (or against), while still finding the details that make the book feel unique.

Designing on spec if trickier, because you're starting with a broad genre. In order to produce covers, I basically had to make up an imaginary book and design a cover for that. I'd start the day by listing four or five weird-ass book concepts, then go to work.

One of them was "Zombie story told in the style of Raymond Carver."

The cover I designed was on sale for approximately three days before I took it down, because that concept plagued me. I had dreams about it.

Which is usually a sign I wanted to write the damn thing myself, even if the concept was so daft that nobody but me truly wanted to see it.

And I did suddenly have a lot of time on my hands now I wasn't working 8 until 6 every day…

ON CARVER

For all the vaunted conflicts between genre and literature, I have a deep affection for Carver's sparse, paired-back dirty realism. Over the years I've taught countless first-year creating writing courses which study his seminal story *So Much Water So Close To Home*, and dipping into his collections are a surefire way of reminding myself why I love the short story form.

On the other hand, I've also lived through countless remixes and homages to his work while teaching university writing courses. There is a certain breed of young writer— often male, often straight—who falls for Carver in their first year of study and spends the next few years trying out variations of his voice and terse misogyny in various assignments.

Take a tour through debut literary collections written by young, white men, and you'll find Carver's influence everywhere.* Which is why the notion of pairing him with the zombie apocalypse tickled me so—it's just so at odds with the cultural space Carver occupies.

If you look closely, you'll see the bones of some of Carver's more famous stories here—where possible, I used the theme or conceits behind one of his tales as the seed, although I aimed to grow something very different from the zombie-trod soil of the Red Rain universe.

OUT PAST THE FENCE

Carver has a knack for writing couples who are in very different places in their lives, and teasing out the tension that creates. It's a nice conceit for an apocalypse story, where you can pair characters who have very different responses to the trauma of society falling apart, then poke at them to see what keeps them together (or drives them apart).

Most of the Red Rain stories are set in or around South East Queensland, often in parts of the world I've lived or visited a bunch, but this is one of the two set further afield. In my head, Janice and Val live up near Cairns, although they moved there after starting down near Brisbane when the rains broke out.

OUR SURVIVAL AND OTHER MYSTERIES

This was the third story I began for this project, but the first to find its way into the world via my Patreon feed. It was written so early, in fact, that the ravages of COVID were still

---

* Arguably, you're also seeing the influence of Carver's editor, Gordon Lish, who approached the writer's work with a heavy hand and imposed a philosophy upon the stories that weren't necessarily in line with Carver's wishes. A full biography and breakdown of this pairing is beyond the scope of this authors note, but digging up commentary and articles about their relationship is a long-standing interest.

pretty fresh in my mind and I was primarily focused on the existential torment inherent in dealing with a massive societal disruption.

It turns out your default Carver protagonist is actually pretty well-equipped to face existential torment. One might argue it's the whole point of Carver's oeuvre.

I remember debating Sam's nickname a lot before letting this story out into the world. The Chin is, obviously, a homage to actor Bruce Campbell and his role as Ash in the Evil Dead.

In general, I'm not a fan of letting parody into an otherwise serious story. It breaks the suspension of disbelief, and relieves tension from the story. Half the art of pulling off a weird concept is playing things straight for the people in the story, even if it's fundamentally absurd.

On the other hand, the central conceit of the Red Rain universe is that zombie stories existed before zombies arrived. Everyone grew up on *Evil Dead* films and *28 Days Later* and *Resident Evil* and *The Walking Dead*.

And I suspect it wouldn't take long for Aussies to start using references to those films as nicknames. It's pretty much how we're wired.

THE MIRACLE MAN EATS

This one owes a huge debt to Carver's story *Fat*, the opening story in the collection *Will You Please Be Quiet, Please?* It's one of two Carver stories I re-read obsessively, a story where the simplicity glosses over the astonishing depths of subtext.

I've tried to capture it's particular magic in one of my own stories before, with varying success, but when I revisited the collection ahead of this project I discovered Carver reads quite differently in a mid-pandemic world. So many of his characters are trapped in a terrible kind of narrative stasis that feels all too familiar after 2020 to 2022.

The Miracle Man Eats is the only story in this collection written without a Queensland setting in mind. For folks who don't live here, it's hard to imagine the sheer size and emptiness of places like Australia, and Queensland is one of our larger states. Driving from the southern border to the tip of Cape York will take you a few days.

It's a different landscape to the bulk of zombie stories that seem to assume a population density, both in the cities but also the sheer number of cities of a certain size. America and Europe—the home to the vast majority of zombie narratives—are dotted with settlements in very close proximity that Australia just doesn't have.

Ergo, this story kept veering back to an American setting. In the Red Rain universe they're probably dealing with the arrival of the undead better than most, and the Miracle Man strikes me as a solution that's liable to emerge from tech culture.

EVERYTHING MUST GO

This story draws an influence from Carver's *Why Don't You Dance?*, and the split perspective that shows us a young woman and an older man's perspectives on the same interaction around a garage sale. I probably wrote more notes after re-reading *Dance* than anything else that appeared in this collection.

While Carver uses his split-perspective narration to shine a light on masculinity and (arguably) make a cultural critique about the predatory nature of men in a culture, the generational divide was really interesting to think about in light of the COVID pandemic.

Zombie stories are—often—about the outbreak and early days of an apocalypse, rather than the generations who grow up in a culture shaped by avoiding and eliminating the undead. The horror of the zombie lies in the idea that it was once recognisably human, and we're conditioned to think of taking life as abhorrent, but how does that change when you arm people and tell them killing zombies is a necessary survival trait?

In the end, it became the story that veered least from structure and conceit of the story that inspired it, largely because I wanted to explore these differences and invert, to a certain extent, the generational power dynamic.

BENEATH THESE TREES, THE DEAD

One reason *So Much Water So Close To Home* is so fascinating to teach is the way students respond to it. It ends on an ambiguity, relying on the momentum of the story to carry you through to a climax that doesn't appear on the stage.

Classe swill spend two hours arguing about which ending they see beyond the final scene in the story. People who like their stories easily digestible and forgettable tend to loathe the lack of a solid, easily understood ending. Some fixate on the gender issues the story deals with, and see undercurrents of threat and domestic violence that other readers miss. Some fall for the language and the spare, coiling terror. Some people just break against it, utterly disturbed by the implications of what a short story could be after spending high school being taught good short stories have a twist ending.

Beneath These Trees, The Dead is my zombie apocalypse tribute to the *So Much Water So Close To Home*. It plays on a similar premise of being tied to someone who may or may not be a threat, coupled with a reluctance to disturb the status quo. Turns out such paranoia lends itself rather naturally to the idea of a zombie contagion, especially after the last few years where we've all seen just how violently some folks react to any curtailing of their activity in the name of pandemic control.

LAST DRINKS

I've long been fascinated by stories by unreliable narrators, and one of my favourites Carver stories is 'What We Talk About When We talk About Love'.

There's an obvious homage in the title of this collection, but also in 'Last Drinks', which takes the same set-up of an unreliable narrator talking about a day of drinking with friends and the stories they tell each other.

This was the story written last, but in the timeline of the Red Rain universe it's taking place very early on. The working title was 'Okay Boomer,' and my interest lay in the transitional nature of big, disruptive events.

I was born in 1977, nominally putting me at the tail end of Generation X but just close enough to Millennials to understand their vibe. For the bulk of my life, the Boomers were pre-eminent shadow over everything, and have shaped the cultural discourse.

They were, in fact, the real world zombie apocalypse of my lifetime: a shambling cohort whose numbers and collective ideology brooked no arguments and devoured all.

It's strange to have lived through a lifetime where they're finally giving away to a younger generation who outnumbers them and thinks very differently. It's fucking glorious to be living through a period where the changing discourse means they're increasingly unable to stay in control because they say so.

ACKNOWLEDGEMENTS

Admittedly, I wouldn't have written these stories without the support and backing of the fine folks at the Eclectic Projects Patreon. For three years, this crew of readers and fans created a safe space to write stories and other projects that were interesting, rather than commercially wise. My sincere thanks go out to Margaret Ball, Kate Eltham, Nicole Strickland, Jodi, Meg Vann, Sally Ball, Jennifer White, Maggie Slater, David Versace, Mark Webb, Seagoat, Kathleen Jennings, Kylie Scott, Tansy Rayner Roberts, Lois Spangler, Ben Francisco, Anja Peerdeman, Trent Jamieson, Catherine Caine, and Stephanie Gunn.

A special thanks to my wife, Sarah "Zazz" Hobday, and Team Write Club: Angela Slatter, Kathleen Jennings, and Joanne Anderton. Also the Sunday Night Cthulhu Crew of Allan Carey, Nicola Logan, Nic Holland, and Adam Norris, who are frequently my sounding board for all things horror and pulp, and may have endured me playing all manner of characters based on semi-famous literary figures over the years.

No doubt, an investigator based on Raymond Carver is coming.

And, finally, thanks to you for picking up my weird-ass zombie book and reading this far. You're awesome.

Peter M. Ball
August 2024
Brisbane, Australia

ABOUT THE AUTHOR

PETER M. BALL is an author, publisher, and RPG gamer whose love of speculative fiction emerged after exposure to *The Hobbit*, *Star Wars*, David Lynch's *Dune*, and far too many games of *Dungeons and Dragons* before the age of 7. He's spent the bulk of his life working as a creative writing tutor, with brief stints as a performance poet, gaming convention organizer, online content developer, non-profit arts manager, GenreCon convener, and d20 RPG publisher.

He's the author of the Miriam Aster series and the Keith Murphy Urban Fantasy Thrillers, three short story collections, and more stories, articles, poems, and RPG material than he'd care to count. He's the brain-in-charge at Brain Jar Press, and resides in Brisbane, Australia, with his partner and two cats.

Peter can be found online at:
www.petermball.com

facebook.com/Petermball
instagram.com/petermball
threads.net/@PeterMBall

ALSO BY PETER M. BALL

DANA VALKYRIE ADVENTURES

White Harbor War

SHORT STORY COLLECTIONS

The Birdcage Heart & Other Strange Tales

Not Quite The End Of the World Just Yet: Short Stories & Strange Futures

These Strange & Magic Things: Short Stories

What We Talk About When We Talk About Brains: The Red Rain Short Stories

Unfamiliar Shores: Stories

KEITH MURPHY URBAN FANTASY THRILLERS

Exile

Frost

Crusade

MIRIAM ASTER CASE FILES

Horn

Bleed

Unicorns, Fey, and a Hardboiled Dame: The Miriam Aster Duology

ESSAY COLLECTIONS

You Don't Want To Be Published & Other Things Nobody Tells You When You First Start Writing

GENREPUNK NINJA ESSAYS

On Heinlein's Rules & The Rise Of The New Pulp Era

Here Be Dragons: Vanity Presses, Scams, And Publishing In The Digital Era